Praise for How

'On the surface the book is a highly competent, creepy little chiller, but beneath, like a silent, bolted and half-dark room, there's a much bigger, equally disconcerting story about the nature of feminine experience. It's an accomplished debut from a writer who shows insight and emotional power'
HILARY MANTEL, Man Booker Prize-winning author of *Wolf Hall* and *Bring Up the Bodies*

'A tense, unnerving debut, told with precision and control. As unsettling as any ghost story'
SIMON LELIC, author of *Rupture* and *The Child Who*

'An impressive debut novel. Here's hoping there'll be more from Emma Chapman'
M. J. HYLAND, Man Booker Prize-shortlisted author of *Carry Me Down* and *This is How*

'The after-effects of the dark and uncomfortable story linger long after the last page . . . a gripping piece of writing where everything is not quite as it seems'
Psychologies

'Wonderfully assured . . . This is a tale of the tricks
repression, denial and memory can play on us . . . Set
in an eerie, purposefully undefined part of Scandinavia,
this is an unnerving, clever read. It's one of those novels
(think *Gone Girl*) with a big twist. Recommended for fans
of S. J. Watson, Rosamund Lupton and Zoe Heller'
Red

'Can be read both as a taut thriller and an allegory
of the female experience in an unhappy marriage . . .
brilliantly convincing. As with Sylvia Plath's *The Bell Jar*,
the narrator's psychological torment contrasts disconcertingly
with the detached language in which it is described.
It makes for a darkly fascinating debut'
Financial Times

'A tremendous book'
Huffington Post

'A taut, economically written and expertly woven thriller –
deceptive in its simplicity and chilling in the claustrophobia
that builds with each successive page. It is also a deeply
unsettling exploration of a fragile mind unravelling . . .
highly assured, powerful and thought-provoking'
Style etc magazine

EMMA CHAPMAN

How To Be a Good Wife

PICADOR

First published 2013 by Picador

First published in paperback 2013 by Picador

This edition first published 2013 by Picador
an imprint of Pan Macmillan, a division of Macmillan Publishers Limited
Pan Macmillan, 20 New Wharf Road, London N1 9RR
Basingstoke and Oxford
Associated companies throughout the world
www.panmacmillan.com

ISBN 978-1-4472-1619-3

1 3 5 7 9 8 6 4 2

A CIP catalogue record for this book is available from
the British Library.

Printed and bound by CPI Group (UK) Ltd, Croydon, CR0 4YY

Visit **www.picador.com** to read more about all our books
and to buy them. You will also find features, author interviews and
news of any author events, and you can sign up for e-newsletters
so that you're always first to hear about our new releases.

For Kate and Keith Chapman
for teaching me everything I know

'Come on my history horses!'

'And below is always the accumulated past, which vanishes but does not vanish, which perishes and remains'

– Marilynne Robinson, *Housekeeping*

1

Today, somehow, I am a smoker.

I did not know this about myself. As far as I remember, I have never smoked before.

It feels unnatural, ill-fitting, for a woman of my age: a wife, a mother with a grown-up son, to sit in the middle of the day with a cigarette between her fingers. Hector hates smoking. He always coughs sharply when we walk behind someone smoking on the street, and I imagine his vocal cords rubbing together, moist and pink like chicken flesh.

I rub the small white face of my watch. Twelve fifteen. By this time, I am usually working on something in the kitchen. I must prepare supper for this evening, the recipe book propped open on the stand that Hector bought me for an early wedding anniversary. I must make bread: mix the ingredients in a large bowl, knead it on the cold wooden worktop, watch it rise in the oven. Hector likes to have fresh bread in the mornings. *Make your home a place of peace and order.*

The smoke tastes of earth, like the air underground. It moves easily between my mouth and my makeshift ashtray: an antique sugar bowl once given to me by Hector's mother. The fear of being caught is like a familiar darkness; I breathe it in with the smoke.

I found the cigarette packet in my handbag this morning underneath my purse. It was disorientating, as if it wasn't my bag after all. There were some cigarettes missing. I wonder if I smoked them. I imagine myself, standing outside the shop in the village, lighting one. It seems ridiculous. I'm vaguely alarmed that I do not know for sure. I know what Hector would say: that I have too much time on my hands, that I need to keep myself busy. That I need to take my medication. Empty nest syndrome, he tells his friends at the pub, his mother. He's always said I have a vivid imagination.

Outside is a clear circle of light. Hector's underpants, shirts and trousers move silently in the breeze. Holding the cigarette upright, the glowing tip towards the ceiling, I notice the red-rimmed edges of my fingernails. A shadow shifts across the table. I see a hand, reaching out: the fingers spread open to take it. It is small, with bitten-down nails, a silver ring gleaming on the index finger. Without thinking, I offer the cigarette, but when I look again the hand is gone. The hairs on my arms rise. I turn quickly, my heart beating, but the room is empty.

With a shaking hand, I stub my cigarette against the delicate china and cross the kitchen. Folding a piece of paper towel around the butt, I wrap it with an elastic band, trying to trap the smell. It still emits the stench of stale smoke. Dropping the sugar bowl into the steaming water in the sink, I hide the cigarette packet in the teapot. I put the paper parcel on the window ledge outside the front door. The air is fresh and cold, like plunging my face and chest into ice water. I will dispose of it later, on my way to the market.

I check my watch again. Twelve twenty-five. I set it every day by the clock on the evening news: it is important for me to know the correct time.

Standing at the open front door on the raised porch, I look out at the dirty stretch of lane. Beyond it, the wide green fields spread towards the edge of the rising valley. The clear blue sky opens up above the darkness of the mountains, and as I look up, I feel dizzy.

The tree at the end of our drive is losing its browning leaves: they pool deliciously at its trunk. I long to hear them crunch under my shoes, to run across the valley and through the dark forest until my lungs burn. The cold wind would lash my face, blowing through my hair: my feet would kick up the dirt. I wouldn't stray from the path.

Holding on to the wooden door, I don't step outside. At one o'clock, I will go to the market. *Your husband belongs in the outside world. The house is your domain, and your responsibility.*

I look at my watch again. Twelve thirty.

Behind the closed front door, it is silent in the house. There is no microwave beeping, no sound of a car door slamming in the drive outside. The washing machine is not even churning: I couldn't scrape together enough for a wash today. The only sound is my breathing, in and out, in and out. The house is always empty now, except for me and sometimes Hector.

The weak midday light slants across the beige carpet. Kylan smiles down from the various pictures on the walls. His first day at school, standing proudly beside Hector's car with his socks pulled up and his new blazer over his arm. In skiing goggles, his face pink and lips rubbery around slightly crooked teeth. Several of him as a baby, his hair sticking up unnaturally and the same gummy smile. I miss him: the stiffness in his crying body, his tense screams, and how he would calm when he found himself in my arms. He has forgotten now, but he felt like this once.

There is only one picture of Hector and me together: our wedding photo. We stand in the church doorway, Hector looking straight at the camera, while I smile up at him. He looks like a husband should: strong and protective and content. If I look closely, I can make out the few grey hairs on his head, the lines around his eyes. My white face is startled by the new light of the churchyard: I was just twenty-one, like a child, my body impossibly slender in the narrow wedding dress. I look happy, but I can't remember if I was. It's so long ago that a dull fog has fallen, and no matter how I grasp, only a few details remain. The particulars of running the house have taken up the space, replacing the old moments. I have a few: Hector's rough hand clasping the top of my arm as we walked through the dark church towards the bright square of daylight. And the feeling of exposure: the eyes of the photographer on my face; Hector's parents standing to one side, watching.

Hector's mother organized everything: she liked things to be done right, and made it quite clear she thought I was too young to understand. Her wedding present to me had been a book: *How To Be a Good Wife*, which she said would teach me everything I needed to know. I still have it somewhere, old, and well-thumbed. I learnt every page by heart.

My apron strings catch on the kitchen door handle and I stop to free myself, noticing a smudge low down on one of the panes of glass. When he was a child, Kylan's finger marks were always there, like ghosts. Now, it looks as if someone with dirty hands has smeared them across the whole bottom panel. I fetch the polish from under the sink, feeling strange that I haven't noticed something so obvious earlier, and rub until the glass comes clean. *You must persevere when cleaning glass, mirrors and silver. The smudges cling on: they do not want to be removed.*

As I scrub at the panel, an image forms like a developing photograph. Hector nervous, standing over me, telling me I have missed a spot, to hurry up, to make sure the house is perfect before his mother arrives. Before we were married, she used to visit on a Sunday to clean the house and cook Hector's dinners for the week ahead, kept in Tupperware containers in the fridge. The first time I met her, Hector had insisted that we clean the house from top to bottom, and though it seemed pointless to me if she was to do it all over again, I did as he asked. Everything needed to be perfect, he repeated, she would notice the slightest mark. It was only later, his mother tutting under her breath as she corrected my work while Hector stood with his fists clenched, that

I saw he had involved me in a lifelong battle between them.

When we heard the doorbell, he pulled off my apron and rubber gloves and we went into the hall together. I see him now, telling me to smile, as if it's happening all over again. The way she looked me up and down, shook my hand and smiled tightly. She asked me where I was from, where I went to school. Did I want children? Hector answered for me. I only nodded.

I hear their voices, through the kitchen door. I am on the other side, out of sight.

'She's very young, Hector.'

'She looks younger than she is.'

'Where did you meet her?'

'We met when I took that holiday to the island.'

'Does she live locally?'

'She's staying here for the time being.'

She breathed in sharply. 'Staying here? How long for?'

Hector sighed. 'I don't know, Mother,' he said. 'Her parents died recently and she doesn't want to be on her own.'

'Well, if you're sure. It just all seems a bit fast. But then, you're not getting any younger.' A pause. 'She's very thin. Is she ill?'

'She's been through a tough time, with her parents. She's a good girl.' There was a silence. 'I'm going to marry her.'

Now, I am here still, standing with my head resting against the closed kitchen door. My heart is hammering. The words seem to have come out of a place I don't go any more. Yet I heard them, as clear as if I was hearing them in that moment. I can't lose the feeling of something in the wrong place.

I go to the tall wooden cabinet in the hall where I keep my china dolls. Hector has bought me a new one each year since we've been married. Twenty-five dolls for twenty-five years. I keep them away from dust, looking at them only through the glass panes, opening the door as little as possible to keep them preserved. Brunettes, blondes and redheads, each face perfect in its own way. My favourite is a blonde-haired doll, sitting in pride of place in the middle row, her perfect curls and pale grey eyes catching the light. I look for her now and for a moment I am confused by what I see. She is facing the wrong way. I feel my throat tighten. Hector knows not to touch my dolls. I wonder if this is his idea of a joke.

Opening the cabinet, I pull on my white gloves. Lifting her out, I tilt her up and down, watching her eyes flick open and shut. I trace her lips with my fingers, always slightly parted, always smiling.

I hear something on the other side of the front door. Startled, I drop her. Looking over my shoulder, I bend to pick her up, my heart thumping. She has landed on her head, but there is no visible damage. There is a noise at the front door again, and my head rings, as if it was me who took the fall. Slipping her back into the cabinet, I walk quickly through to the kitchen, shutting the door behind me. I slide a knife from the draining board and wait.

The front door creaks open, and then shuts. Steps travel slowly across the hallway. I let my breath escape.

I open my eyes. It's Hector, standing on the other side of the kitchen doorway, watching me.

We watch each other through the thick glass panels: we don't smile. At the bottom, I see his brown leather brogues, the laces tied. In the middle, his corduroy trousers are pressed stiffly, his hands in his pockets. At the top: his calm blue eyes; the steady line of his mouth, slightly curved down at the corners; his greying hair brushed sparsely. He has deep creases in the skin of his cheeks.

He sees: slippers, the bottom of my black everyday trousers. The neat red apron, a pale pink cashmere jumper, the knife glinting by my side. My make-up-less face, no doubt severe in the bright daylight. My hair tied into a neat dull chignon at the back of my head, dark blonde with the beginnings of grey. *Before he arrives home, freshen your make-up; put a ribbon in your hair.*

I risk a smile: as he smiles back, the lines around his eyes shift. Now that he's here, I feel better, and almost silly that I worked myself up before, thinking someone was breaking in.

I turn, slipping the knife under the surface of the water in the sink. Hector opens the door.

'Hi,' he says.

I glance at the kitchen clock. Twelve thirty-five.

'You're home early,' I say.

Hector nods. 'No classes this afternoon,' he says.

I have to look away from him, down into the water. I begin to wash the knife. The soap slips off the gleaming metal as I slide it onto the draining board.

Hector is still standing there, watching me.

'How was your day?' I ask.

'It smells of smoke in here,' he says.

'I burnt some toast.' I keep my hands below the surface of the water. 'Have you been touching my dolls?'

'What do you mean?' His voice is slow, careful.

'My dolls. Someone has been moving them.'

He comes towards me; I stay still. He raises his hand and I feel the warmth of his palm on my forehead, dry and papery.

'Are you feeling all right?' he asks.

'I'm fine,' I say, opening my eyes.

'Not still feeling sick?'

'No.'

'Have you taken your medication?'

I shake my head.

Hector opens the cupboard above the sink. I hear the rattle of the bottle.

'Open your mouth,' he says.

I let my jaw go slack. The pink pill moves past my eye line, and when I feel it on my tongue, I swallow. He gestures, and I open my mouth again.

He checks. 'Good girl,' he says, putting his hand at the base of my neck. 'I'm going to have a shower.' He turns to leave.

I pick up the knife from the draining board and begin to wash it again.

Without looking up, I listen to him climb the stairs. Once I am sure he is gone, I let my legs go, sinking against the kitchen counter. Cupping a hand to my mouth, I expel the small pill, letting it drop into a gap between the skirting board and the floor. It has been so long now since I remember actually swallowing one.

I haven't mentioned it to Hector. He would want to have a discussion, to remind me of how I get without them. Just the thought of it gives me a headache and I put my hands up to my temples, rubbing at them, pushing the pain away.

The last time I stopped taking my pills, Kylan must have been eleven or twelve. He had just started getting the bus from the end of the lane with Vara, his friend from the farm. I found that now he was away more, at senior school with its additional after-school activities, there was less for me to do in the house. When he was younger, I was so busy, I barely had time to think: he was always there, wanting me. But now, there was only the washing, ironing, dusting, and making his dinner. I had already had time to make stacks of stockpiled meals, waiting in the freezer. I started to look for the shadows of dust that fell on things.

But it wasn't just that there was less to do and the house was so quiet. I felt him slipping away from me. In the evenings, I would meet him from the bus and ask him questions as we walked home, but he wanted to talk less and less. He kept more to himself, and I missed the shape of his child's body, grasping after me. One day, he told me he didn't need me to collect him from the bus stop any more. I said that I liked to, but he insisted that he could walk down the lane by himself. Hector said it was normal, that he was growing up. But it was easy for him to say: Kylan had started talking to him more.

So I stopped taking my pills because I wanted something to happen. I suppose I wanted him to notice me again. I almost welcomed the weariness that came without them: the heavy darkness I dimly remembered which begin to follow me around again. I would be doing a job in the kitchen, and before I knew it, I would be out on the porch step, numbly watching the horizon. Kylan would come in from school and find me there. Dinner was never ready, and his bed hadn't been made. Sometimes I cried without understanding why, and couldn't stop even with Kylan's warm body against mine, his hair against my nose. I remember clinging on to him, whispering in his ear, waiting for it to pass.

Eventually, Kylan told Hector, and he got it out of me that I had stopped taking my pills. He said it wasn't good for Kylan to have to do everything himself. *Children need order and routine: to be surrounded by stability.* That's when he started to check up on me.

'Some people just need a little help, Marta,' he said. 'It's nothing to be ashamed of.'

And now, Kylan isn't here again and the silent house makes me want to scream. He isn't coming back this time, and there's no reason for me to hold it together. There is even less to do these days. Skipping my pills is like an experiment, one I allow to continue because in my worst moments, I long for something bad to happen. If it does, maybe Kylan will come back and help to take care of me.

And I like the warm, strong feeling I get from fooling Hector. It is better than feeling nothing at all.

Thinking I hear him on the landing, I make myself get up and take out the ingredients for bread. I stand, watching the neat packages of flour, yeast, butter, waiting for the whirr of the bathroom fan, the sounds of the shower. I want to seem busy, but the pressure of Hector above me makes me feel tired and after some time, I put the ingredients away again, into their proper places.

I check my watch: five minutes to one. In the hallway, Hector's mahogany walking stick is propped against the wall. A recent addition, since his knee operation, a reminder that he is getting old. The doctor said it was only temporary, but I have a feeling Hector likes it, that it makes him feel distinguished.

I pick up the bundle of letters lying on the doormat and dust the front of them. On one of the envelopes there is a faint brown smudge, which I ignore.

The names on the letters do not seem familiar.

Mrs Marta Bjornstad. Mr and Mrs Hector Bjornstad. Mr and Mrs H. C. Bjornstad.

Before I leave the house, I put all the letters, even the

ones with just my name, into a pile on the hall table for Hector. *Let your husband take care of the correspondence and finances of the household. Make it your job to be pretty and gay.*

When my watch reads one o'clock, I pull on my red tartan coat and navy headscarf and leave the house.

2

I drive into town. The greens rush past the car window: it has been a verdant autumn with plenty of rain. Verdant. I wonder where I picked up that word.

The sun is at its brightest: it is the middle of the day. The road runs along our edge of the valley, and from the slight height I can see for miles. The sky spreads above the curve below, which is marked with patches of denser green where the mossy forest lies. I can see the traces of the roads, white crisscrossed lines in the sunlight, running around the houses and cutting through the fields. The distant mountains rise higher and darker, surrounding us: shadowed blue-green masses capped with white snow.

I make out the beginnings of the fjord, spreading across the bottom of the valley. Whenever I round the bend and see it hanging there, I am reminded of an early tour Hector gave me, just after the wedding. We were on bicycles, though I don't recall where mine came from or when it appeared in the house. I remember I didn't have a helmet and Hector had to lend me his: the silver hairs around his temples standing out in the sunlight. He seemed so old to me even then, though he was forty-one when we married, younger than I am now.

As I drive the same road we cycled, I tell myself again what he has always said about that day. About how happy we were. All the way, I could feel him behind me: I listened to the sound of his bicycle chain engaging as he cycled close and then fell back a little. The sun was behind us, and Hector's long shadow fell over mine as we rode along. I looked at our shadows intertwined on the tarmac. That is my husband's shadow, I told myself. I am his wife. I remember thinking that having Hector there made me safe.

Continuing through the valley, wooden houses pepper the roadside and spread sparsely across the land. Like Kylan's old toy houses: reds, blues and yellows, painted garishly to counter the perpetual winter darkness. Further up, on the steep sides of the hills, the houses cling precariously. I imagine the black water of the fjord rising, washing them all away, sending splintered wood travelling through the rocky precipices towards the sea.

Soon, the sky will begin to darken again as the winter

looms. Too little to notice at first, until the world is dim and we are wandering around with our eyes half closed.

I drive slowly along the edge of the water as I approach the village. The mirror of water doubles the size of the sky. Something flashes in the corner of my eye, and turning my head I see a child running away from me along the path by the fjord, her blonde hair catching the sun. She moves fast, her arms and legs wild. I look to see if she's playing a game, if there is anyone chasing her, but she's alone at the lakeside. Although she must be fifty metres away, I can hear her breaths, in and out, in and out, louder and louder until they fill the car.

A loud noise outside makes me jump. I have come to a halt in the middle of the road, and behind me, a farm vehicle is glaring, its horn willing me to drive on. As I do, I look again, but the girl is gone.

I park near the white wooden church, standing neatly at the water's edge, surrounded by the flagged cemetery. Sitting in the car, I watch the gravestones standing in the shadow of the trees, grouped together. The annoyance of Hector in the house when he is not supposed to be has followed me across the bright valley. He fills the white walls, shrinking the space until it feels too small. I know it is not my place to ask questions: Hector will have a good reason. *Never question his authority, for he always does what is best for the family, and has your interests at heart.*

Getting out of the car, I look back just once to check it is still there. The grey spire of the church stands black and clear against the sky, sharp enough to cause a rupture.

I pass the old town hall with its white wooden-slatted exterior, freshly painted every year. On the front of the building, there's a clock: the gold roman numerals glimmer in the sunlight. One twenty-five. The large yellow doors have been pushed open and the dim lobby gapes, the dusty light shifting into darkness.

The blue post office on the opposite side of the road is a smaller building, less imposing. It is almost like a house with its wooden veranda and white benches where elderly people sit in the summertime. I try to imagine Hector and me sitting there, hand in hand, but I can't.

Kylan's old school is beyond the main stretch, an old barn-like gymnasium to the rear. Beyond that are the two hotels: the grand old one right on the water, and the less imposing inn-like one that acts as the village pub. I never go beyond the hotels: I haven't in the whole time I've lived here. These are my limits: the hotels on this side of the fjord, and the doctor's surgery on the other.

I walk along the narrow road to the market, catching glimpses of the water through the scattered buildings.

Many of the stalls have blue tarpaulin canopies to keep out the rain, casting the people in a strange light. Some of them smile at me, but even after all these years, I am still an outsider. Not like Hector, who has always lived here.

There is a group of women standing by one of the vegetable stalls, chatting with a man who is a farmer and one of the town councillors. He wears the uniform of the men in the valley: a battered all-weather jacket, Wellingtons and brown work trousers. His tough, lined face shifts as he smiles and raises his hand. The women whisper, pretending not to see me. They wear bright practical coats and hiking boots, their hair protruding from woollen hats. Robust women, who help run the farms and bring up hardy families. They saw me, in the early days, a thin girl from the city in her new clothes, and that is how they still see me, though I have lived here now for most of my life.

I reach the pub, where most of the village congregates in the evenings: catching up on the farming gossip and news of children who have grown up and moved away. Hector had been a regular before me, and I remember we went down together one evening. Standing here now, by the doors, I feel strangely nervous, as if it is that night again. I repeat what Hector has always told me: what a lovely evening we had, how nice it was to be one of two, a couple, at last. But the jangling of nerves is familiar and seems to bring things into focus: the sudden image of picking at the sleeve of the new jumper Hector had bought me, a new haircut feeling all wrong. I was worried about all the people, and about how it was best to behave. I knew he wasn't sure if I was ready, if I was quite well enough yet.

The pub was warm and smelt of frying fish. Hector entered ahead of me, greeted warmly by a group near the entrance. He stood up straighter then, his shoulders less slouched. There were people everywhere, pushing up against the walls, crowding in at the bar. They turned to look when we entered, and I saw them start to talk. I couldn't get my hands to stop shaking so I shoved them into my pockets, looking down at my bony legs, the clothes that were too big. Every time I moved my head, I saw the dark edges of my new haircut.

An older man, around Hector's age, sidled over to us and put his arm around Hector's back.

'So, this is your new woman?' he asked, grinning at me. I tried to smile.

'This is Marta,' Hector said.

I held my hand out.

'Got some manners, this young one,' he said.

Hector smiled. 'She's well trained.' They both laughed.

'I suppose Hector's told you about me,' he said. 'I'm the village doctor. Where are you from, Marta?' he asked.

I looked at Hector. 'I'm from the city,' I said.

'A city girl?' the man said, raising his eyebrows. 'You must think we're very backward around here.'

I smiled and shook my head. The man was waiting.

'She doesn't say much,' he said to Hector. 'But I suppose that's how we like them.' He leaned in close and I told myself not to flinch at his beery breath. 'I wish my wife was more like you.'

A woman appeared behind him. Child-bearing hips, that's what I thought when I saw her. I could see the angry red veins through the transparent skin of her cheeks. Her eyes shone, and her hair was glossy brown with a few spindly grey hairs. She looked me up and down, then leaned in and gave the man a kiss on the cheek.

'Speak of the devil,' the man said, grinning at me.

'What's he been saying?' she said, putting her hand on her hip. Her fingernails were short and neat, and her wedding ring looked as if it had always been on her finger.

'Only how wonderful you are, my darling,' he said. 'So wonderful, in fact, that I'd like to get you a drink.'

The woman waved her glass at him, ice cubes tinkling. 'I have a drink, *darling*,' she said.

He winked. 'You can always have another.' He turned to Hector. 'She's much nicer to me when she's had a few. Want a drink?'

Hector asked for a beer. 'And for you?' the man said to me.

'Water, please,' I answered.

He sidled away towards the bar.

The woman turned back to us.

'We haven't seen you around here for a while, Hector,' she said. 'Did you get the renovations finished?'

'Finally,' he said. 'Thanks again, by the way. Everyone was so helpful.'

'Don't mention it,' she said, putting her hand on Hector's arm.

There was a silence, surrounded by the restless noise of the pub.

'Well, I've never known Hector to bring a girl to the pub before,' she said. 'We'd begun to give up hope. Must be love.'

Hector blushed then, and I felt my cheeks redden too. 'Good on you,' the woman said, laughing. She put her arm around me: it was warm and heavy. 'About time too.'

The other man was calling to Hector across the room:

he wanted help carrying the drinks from the bar. When Hector left to join him, the woman turned to me.

'So how did you two meet?' she asked.

I looked at the woman's bony red ear, inches away from my mouth. I could feel Hector's eyes on me from where he was standing with the other men. His face was serious. I didn't want to do the wrong thing, to cause a scene and embarrass him when he had been so kind to me. When I tried to think back to meeting Hector, there was nothing there, like trying to see past a thick curtain. I remembered the words he had told me.

'We met on holiday by the sea,' I said. 'I was swimming, and Hector saved me from drowning.'

As I said it, I could see the water spreading heavily towards the horizon, and feel the weight of it around my nose, in my ears and throat.

The woman's eyes widened. 'Oh, how romantic,' she said. 'Makes our story sound pretty boring. We met right here, in this pub.'

I felt Hector's hand on the base of my spine.

'Time to go home,' he said.

Even now, the light is beginning to dim behind the buildings, casting long shadows across the road. Standing still, I try to slow my breathing. I check my watch. I couldn't say where I have been for the last few minutes.

The village women have gone now, and I stare at the spot where they were standing, watching the shoes of people passing. Comfortable, practical walking shoes, with good grip; trousers tucked into socks. Hiking boots for the more serious rambler. The plimsolls of tourists, wet-edged with dew. Fur-lined snow boots, though it isn't cold enough for them yet. Eventually, the market comes back into focus, and I begin to walk.

Noticing the traces of frost in the fishmonger's window, I pull my scarf closer around my neck and slip into the shop. There is a big wooden fish on the wall with a yellow eye that watches me. The fishmonger is serving a young mother with a pushchair. The child inside looks up at me as he sucks his fist, his eyelashes like insect legs brushing against his cheeks.

The fishmonger removes some glass-bodied halibut from the display. He turns to the white counter to prepare it. As I watch him slice down the edge of the fish, I long to make a halibut stew for Kylan: his favourite.

There is a blonde girl in her late teens behind the counter, helping the fishmonger, her hair glistening in the electric light. She fetches the boning and disembowelling tools for him, waits as he works, then wraps the fish in waxed paper and hands it to the lady with the toddler. Her fingernails are bitten down, red and sore: I can't take my eyes off her hands. As she glances up and half smiles at the lady, I see her black eyeliner. Something cold shifts in my stomach, passing over my skin and making the hairs rise. I keep my eyes on the traces of fishy wetness that shine on the ground.

I hear the man behind me tapping his foot on the linoleum. I look back and he stares straight through me, his mouth hidden under his beard. The shop feels too warm and too small. I turn quickly towards the door, shoving past the lady with the pushchair. She tuts, but I keep moving, back along the stretch of market stalls, feeling the cold air against my cheeks.

My mind is humming. Some of the sellers rub their rough red hands together. When I ask for vegetables, they pretend not to hear me. I can see the smiles that turn up the corner of their mouths.

As I walk back to the car empty-handed, I think about the fishmonger's hands. I wonder if his wife and children have become used to them: to the smell of the sea as he leans past them to reach into a cupboard above their heads, or tucks them into their beds at night. I wonder if they ever flinch. Perhaps they all live inside the smell, no longer aware of its presence.

Passing the last of the houses before the church, the road ahead continues through the valley. The water is close on the other side of the buildings, and I feel its presence there, its depth. I am alone now, moving further away from the centre of the town. Back into the open space between here and home.

I tell myself I'm walking towards Hector in the red-brick schoolhouse on the other side of the water, though I know that he is not there. I like to think of him, dressed up in his corduroys and a blazer. Sometimes, I see myself as one of his students at the back of the class. The dull morning light is breaking through the classroom blinds and onto the blackboard. It is marked with some incomprehensible formula, which is actually the opposite: as clear and logical as Hector's mind. He sits behind his desk, pen poised amongst the hush of working students, or stands in front of the class, arms folded, waiting for the little moments of realization to fall about the room like feathers.

It is his place: the place where he can prove that he is right. It follows that if you take a logical argument step by step to its conclusion, there can be no grey areas. On that blackboard, in that room, there is right or wrong, black or white. *If the premises of a valid argument are true, then its conclusion must also be true. It is impossible for the conclusion of a valid argument to be false if its premises are true.* These are the things he teaches.

Hector says I could never take one of his classes, that my brain doesn't work the same way as his. I'm not logical; I can't see things as they really are. He says a lot of women are like me: unable to see the wood for the trees. I have other strengths, he says, though he never tells me what they are.

As I pull out onto the road, I think about him, in the house. The orange light on the dashboard reads 3:25. It is so strange, for him not to be following his usual routine. I feel my hands begin to shake on the steering wheel as I picture him: pacing in his study, messing up the kitchen. He has tipped the delicate balance that is holding us together.

3

I drive the familiar stretch of road again. Edging the darkness of the jagged trees along the top of the valley, I notice the sky is beginning to dim, as if its strength is failing. The clocks went back last week and we are losing the light. It happens gradually every year, the slip into winter. Unless you are diligent, it can creep up on you, leaving you in flat darkness. A never-changing nothing that makes my teeth ache.

The pressure of the town eases as I drive on. To my left, the dense forest begins. Out of the corner of my eye, I see a flash of pink between the trees, but when my head turns, it is gone. I reach to switch the radio on.

After a few songs have passed, I hear myself singing along softly. The tune isn't one I recognize, but the words keep coming, filling the car. After a while, I put my hand to my mouth. It is closed. The voice keeps singing. I jerk the wheel, trying to get away from her, and before I know it, I have swerved onto the grass verge and my foot has slipped from the accelerator. The engine has cut out. The car is full of silence and the screen of the radio is blank.

I look ahead at the empty grey road sloping upward, listening for the voice, but it doesn't return. Though I tell myself it was my imagination, something in me longs to hear it. Nothing happens. I look out over the valley to my right: this is the highest point of the drive home. I can see the water spreading behind me around the hills. From here, the spire of the white church is a pinprick, and I remember how dangerous it looked when I stood directly below it, looking up at the sky.

There is nothing left to do but continue, so I turn on the car engine, pushing my juddering foot down onto the accelerator, hearing the revs echo through the space.

Eventually, I turn into our lane. It's long and narrow, rounding a bend so that our house is out of sight from the main road. The house sits back, lower down, hidden behind the skeletons of the trees, its oversized roof sloping towards the ground. The white shutters look dirty and a collection of old leaves have blown onto the wide raised porch.

I watch as the front door opens and a woman walks out onto the stone doorstep. She carries a child on her hip, a boy with blond hair, and she is wearing my red apron, splattered with what looks like cake batter. She smiles as she puts the little boy on the ground and begins to sweep the leaves. I hear her humming to herself. The little boy watches her with wide eyes. He reaches his arms out to her, and when she is finished, she scoops him up and runs back into the house with him. I can hear their laughter intertwining. Then the door closes and the house is as it was.

Walking up the steps to the front door, I can see my breath. The rolled-up parcel is no longer on the window ledge. I try to see where Hector is in the house; none of the downstairs lights are on. I slide the key into the lock.

In the kitchen, I open the fridge door: the mix of colours and the tight squeeze of everything inside make me feel warm. I couldn't fit anything else in if I tried, but I still like to go to the market at one o'clock every day. It is a habit I can't seem to break.

I check the clock.

Normally, I would be expecting Hector back soon: I would be preparing the dinner. Since our honeymoon, I don't remember him taking a single day off, or coming home before the usual time.

I wipe down the kitchen surfaces. That's ten more minutes gone. Then I check the teapot. The cigarettes are not there.

The kitchen table is strewn with empty envelopes: Hector must have opened the post. Scooping them into a pile, I open the bin lid to throw them away.

The cigarette packet is in the bin. Gingerly, I pick it out. It's damp, the cigarettes inside soaked through: they've been run under the tap. A couple have avoided the water. I slide them out and put the packet back where I found it.

Slowly, I walk through the kitchen and up the stairs, looking down the long dark corridor towards Hector's study, listening for him. There's a bar of light under the door: a shadow moves across it. I walk to our bedroom, leaning down on my side of the bed and sliding the two dry cigarettes under the mattress, feeling the springs stretch.

When I pull my hand back out from under the mattress, it won't come. It's as if something is holding it there and I can't get away. My arm is drawn further in; I feel a pain at the tip of my finger and cry out. Then, without warning, I am released and thrown backwards.

Reaching over, I turn on my bedside light. My index fingernail is torn right down: a line of blood begins to appear.

I lift the mattress up with both hands and peer underneath it, but there is nothing there. Looking again at my finger, I wonder if I did that to myself and have only just noticed it. All the fingers are bitten, but this is the worst one. I pull myself up, wipe my hands on my trousers, and return to the brightness of the kitchen.

I run my hands under the warm tap for a long time, dousing them with soap and scrubbing. The water gets hotter and hotter, until my index finger stings at the raw edges, but I hold them there, until they are clean again.

4

We have lamb casserole for dinner. *After a hard day at work, your husband will want a hearty meal to replenish his spirits.* I fill my biggest saucepan with chunks of steaming brown lamb, carrots, onions and mushrooms, submerged in thick gravy.

When the casserole is bubbling gently, I pour myself a glass of wine and stand by the patio windows. The sky is dark blue. I can still make out the traces of the washing line, and the thick outline of the hedgerows at the edge of the garden. Beyond that, the mountains loom. My watch reads five thirty-six, and it is already night.

In the old days, Kylan would eat at five thirty, ravenous from school. I would pile food high on his plate and call him in. Standing here, by the windows, I would ask him about school, and he would chatter away about football and maths and biology and how much homework he had. When he was finished, he would return to the television, leaving his plate for me to clear away.

Before that, when he was a baby, I would feed him myself. We had an old green high chair with a blue plastic tray that Kylan loved to slap his fat little hands on. I would tie a bib around his neck, making him laugh when it tickled, and pull up the chair nearest to him, pulling faces as I fed him. Even when it wasn't easy, when he was in a bad mood and didn't want to play, I loved every second I was with him.

*

At exactly seven thirty, I stand at the bottom of the stairs and call for Hector. His name is a harsh word, sharp in my throat, like machinery breaking down. When I first heard it, I imagined it was a strong name: the name of a protector, a warrior, a fortress. I was right, I suppose.

I mound huge hills of mashed potato onto our plates, drown them in casserole, and garnish them with trees of broccoli. There is still enough food left in the pan to feed us twice over.

I sit at the table, not eating, watching curls of steam rise from my plate. I can picture him in his study, his navy slippers resting on the edge of his faux mahogany desk. His reading glasses on, half-moons, glinting as his eyes shift across the page. He always finishes his chapter.

Never hurry or nag him along. His time is precious, and must be treated as such.

I am being punished, of course, for the cigarette. I pour myself a second glass of wine.

I'm hungry. The cigarette was all I had for my lunch, and the tender lumps of lamb are almost irresistible.

Always wait for him before you begin eating: he should always come first.

I hear him moving in his study. Getting up from his desk. Putting his book down. Walking across the floor. Opening and shutting the door.

Now he is going into the bathroom.

The walls in this house are thin. I almost laugh to myself, looking at the table that I have carefully laid. There is even a candle.

I pick up my fork.

As I look at the steaming plate of food before me, the smell spreads through my body, filling up my head. There doesn't seem to be room to breathe.

Looking to my left at the wide patio doors, I see the body of a sturdy middle-aged woman, a wine glass at her side. One of her hands clasps a fork, the other rests on the wooden table, her wedding ring glinting.

I remember watching myself before, years ago, my static reflection caught in the car window as we rushed through countryside, following a river. We were off on our first holiday together. It wasn't long before the wedding and it was summer. We have always told people we met on that trip, but we had met before, when I was ill and Hector had taken care of me. We thought it would be best not to tell people about that: it only made them ask questions about the past. Hector didn't want me to be embarrassed, or to have to talk about my parents: he knew it upset me.

We ducked through various valleys on the long journey east. Hector and I often talk of this holiday we took, and we remember it fondly. I have a few details I return to, like the car skimming through the green land. When I think hard, I can feel the wind whipping my hair back on the ferry across to the island, where cars are forbidden. Trying to catch my breath on the short, steep walk from the port. Peeking behind us at the water stretching towards the horizon, the sun turning the sea to molten orange. Of the house, I remember a smooth pine table at which we ate some bread and cheese, and the green blind that was pulled down over the bathroom window. Hector tells me we went for dinner one night in a restaurant along the harbour: we both ate lobster, which was a special treat. There are photos of us, sitting in the fading sunlight. In one of them we are holding hands.

As I sit here now at the kitchen table, other things start to show themselves. I remember the smell of a musty bedroom, and the strange silence all around us. It must have been the morning as there was light at the window and I could hear birdsong. The mound of Hector's body asleep next to me, his breathing. I listened for a long time, afraid he was still awake. Once he began to snore, I climbed out of the bed and crept out into the hallway.

From the window, the water shimmered in the new light. The sun made the wooden staircase glow, breaking across the floor and furniture of the living room in heavy blocks. There was the heady smell of pine. A step creaked and I stopped. After a minute of stillness, I kept going. I found the key to the cottage. Slowly, as silently as I could, I stepped across the old brown kitchen tiles, unlocked the back door and followed the path through the expanse of rocky land.

I can see the building: near the water, perched on the edge of the sloping brown and red rocks. Behind it, the dark green forest began. The rocks were splattered with white lichen, alien red shrubbery growing from dark places in between. Stumbling a little, each step measured, I made my way. At every moment, I saw myself fall, my skull smashing like a watermelon onto the rocks.

Ahead, the sea stretched flatly in the deserted cove. There were rocky islands not far out, breaking the surface, making it seem shallow: a flooded plain. I imagined the grey slate roofs of houses below the surface, covered by a sudden flood: tables, chairs, plates, cups and saucers, floating above their place.

Hearing the waves breaking and smelling the sea, I began to feel awake. I pulled off my clothes and walked along a wooden jetty, settling myself on the edge. The air was fresh against my bare skin, and without thinking I dropped into the water.

I swam down, tasting salt, the water rushing about my ears. Pushing back with my arms, I went as deep as I could. A strange blue blur filled my eyes, twisted by the light from above. My head felt lighter, my limbs loosened in their sockets. It was calm and quiet at last. The surface moved further and further away as my breath tightened across my chest. I watched it go, the shafts of sunlight blurring and dimming. I shut my eyes.

Just when everything was perfectly still, a shadow fell. There were hands, sharp under my armpits, and my body was pulled upwards, rushing towards the surface. I kicked to get away but the world came into glimmering focus, the line of the horizon rocking. My body was too weak to break free: all I wanted was to return to the coolness beneath the water. I struggled but was still dragged backwards. My scream rang out through the morning air. Immediately, the hands disappeared.

'Ssshh,' a voice said.

I breathed in sharply, my breaths falling over each other, unable to catch up. I could see the jetty now, only a few metres away.

Hector was floating next to me: his hair slicked back, his wide blue eyes as dark as the water below the surface.

He pulled himself onto the platform, reaching his arm out for me. With the sun behind him, he was little more than a shadow. I felt the strength in his brown arms as he lifted me. His body was taut and muscular, the shadow of dark hairs on his chest sparkling with trapped water.

'What the hell are you doing?' he said.

I sank onto the wooden floor, unable to catch my breath. The sun was too bright. When I could finally open my eyes, he was gone, walking away from me along the jetty. I was shivering. I heard something behind me: he was coming back, holding a big blue towel open. Pressing it around my body, he sat down beside me.

He looked into the dark water. 'What were you doing?' he said again.

'I came for a swim,' I said eventually.

I could feel him looking down at my naked body, my

frail limbs, and I pulled them up to my chest under the towel.

He took hold of my narrow wrist, his hand tight. 'Marta, you need to be honest with me. I know you weren't swimming.'

I looked down at his hand, tightening around my skin.

'I thought you were starting to feel better,' he said. 'That staying with me was helping.'

He looked so hurt, and I wanted to make it better. 'It was,' I said. 'I just wanted a swim.'

'I thought I could make you happy.'

I tried to smile. 'I am happy.'

'I don't know what else I can do,' he said. 'You've started taking your pills again. You're putting on weight. You're much calmer than you were.'

'I'm fine, Hector, honestly.'

He looked out across the sea. 'Am I doing something wrong?' he said, almost to himself. 'I've done everything I can.'

I shook my head. 'No,' I said. 'You've been so good to me.'

'It's because I love you, Marta,' he said. 'I just want to take care of you.'

'Sometimes I just feel alone,' I said.

'But you're not,' he said. 'I'll always be here.'

I didn't say anything.

'Do you still miss them?'

Slowly, I nodded my head.

He looked so sad. I tried to think what to say to make it all right again, when he turned to me.

'If we get married, you won't ever have to be on your own again. We can start a new family together. Perhaps it will help you forget.'

I looked down at his hand around my wrist. Red blotches had started to rise around his fingers.

'Would you like that?' he said.

I couldn't answer. He saw me looking at my wrist and removed his hand. When he saw the red marks, he traced them with his finger.

'You're so delicate,' he said.

I rested my head on his shoulder, breaking eye contact. 'I'm so tired all the time,' I said.

'We don't have to have a big thing: I know you're not up to that. Just a small ceremony. I'll get Mother to organize it when we get back.'

I was still shivering.

'Let's go in,' he said. 'I'll give you a bath. And next time you feel like swimming, I can come with you. You shouldn't have gone out alone.' I let him rub my arms with the towel. 'Marta,' he said, the name sounding strange to me. 'Look at me.' I lifted my eyes slowly over the dark stubble on his chin; across his cheeks, tanned from the summer sun, to his waiting eyes. 'I've only just found you. Don't leave me again. Promise me.'

His eyes were wide with something.

'I promise,' I said. I tried to stand up then, but the light was bright all around me, and I fell back, shutting my eyes. He stood up and held out his hand. I paused, then took it.

He pulled me up, putting his arm around my shoulder for a moment. It was wet and heavy; it felt wrong there.

I watched the water fall from my hair, forming circles on the wood near his hairy toes. Then we walked back towards the house.

In the kitchen, my fork clatters onto the table. I breathe in and out. I know that Hector saved me from drowning on that trip: we've told people the story for years. It is light, romantic, and people love to hear it. But this version is different. It's as if I am listening to a familiar song played slightly out of tune. That heaviness I felt then, a sickness turning, is here with me now.

I have waited long enough, I think, digging my fork into the casserole and shovelling down mouthful after mouthful, barely chewing. I want to stop and wait for Hector, the guilt hot in my cheeks, but I am too hungry.

He is coming down the stairs, across the new carpet we had put in after Kylan went to the city three months ago. I make myself put down my fork and swallow.

I see the navy blue velvet of his slippers, then the bottom half of his corduroyed legs. He is slow, holding on to the handrail to protect his knee. My stomach dips. He comes in, half smiles, and sits in his place. He looks at the food, at my half-eaten plateful. I keep my eyes on the table. He picks up his knife and fork. I pick up mine. He begins to eat. I do too. We eat in silence. I concentrate on my lamb. It's perfectly cooked.

Let him talk first. Remember that his topics of conversation are more important than yours.

He always breaks the silence if I leave it long enough.

'How was the market?' he asks.

'Good,' I say. 'The butcher was busy.'

'He's a good butcher. You can trust his meat.'

Hector says this as if he is an expert on butchering practices. Or as if he goes to the butcher himself.

'Yes,' I say.

We continue eating.

Remember always to be bright and cheerful: a breath of fresh air.

'Would you like some wine?' I ask, gesturing at the half-empty bottle on the table.

'No, thank you,' he says. He looks at me. 'Make that your last one. You know you're not supposed to drink with your pills.'

I keep my eyes on the table. Remembering the candle, I take the lighter out. The table glows.

'Where did you get that lighter?' Hector asks.

'It's the one from the kitchen drawer,' I say.

The accusing look in his eyes falters.

'It's been in there for years, for lighting birthday candles and things,' I continue.

He takes a mouthful of lamb and chews it slowly, still examining his plate.

'Why was it in your pocket?' he says.

'I was going to light the candle,' I say, looking at him calmly.

'Oh,' he says.

I scrape my plate clean.

I watch Hector eat, cutting his food up into small pieces before eating them, chewing slowly and methodically. This is rare for a man. *Better good manners than good looks.*

As I watch his mouth, I see another row of teeth moving faster and faster, shovel, swallow, shovel, swallow.

No chewing. As he smiles, I see the food between them, on his tongue, imagine it travelling down his throat. I shut my eyes, thinking for a moment I am going to be sick.

'Marta?' Hector says. 'Are you OK?'

I open my eyes. A piece of lamb glistens on his fork. I swallow. 'I'm fine,' I say. 'I just ate too quickly.'

Take small mouthfuls of food, like a baby bird, and make sure to chew daintily with your mouth closed.

I wait for him to look away.

5

After dinner, Hector goes to the living room, leaving me to clear up.

As I wipe the green sponge over the plates at the sink, the taste of bare china fills my mouth, cold and hard. My teeth ache deep into the gums and I clench them together, waiting for the feeling to pass. I take a swig from the wine bottle, swallowing to clear the taste in my mouth. When I pull the bottle away, it is empty.

Opening the bin to scrape in the leftover broccoli, I step backwards: it's filled with wet hair. I think I see something move: for a moment I think it is an animal, and I am about to call to Hector. But when I look back, there is nothing there. The edge of the cigarette packet is visible, underneath a pile of envelopes. I slam the bin lid down, hard.

Reaching into the cupboard above my head, I pull out the small orange pot of pills. I hold it in my hands, touching the peeling edge of the label. *Marta Bjornstad. Take three daily with food.* No, I think. I won't.

The pills go back into their place. Opening a new bottle of wine, I pour myself a glass and go through to the living room.

The clock above the mantelpiece reads 8:15. Hector has turned on the lamps and the room glows warmly. The thick cream curtains are drawn at the bay window facing the lane.

He is lying on the sofa, propped up on one of the ivory cushions, his arms bent behind his head. One slipper hangs off his foot. His face is soft: his eyes are shut, his chest moving slowly and rhythmically. The creases on his brow have disappeared and he almost looks happy. Like a boy. I look at the grey hairs around his temples, his thinning hairline. He isn't a boy, I think; he's getting to be an old man now. As I watch him, listening to his laboured breathing, I feel a familiar rush of pity for him. There are twenty years between us.

His eyes open, and I am caught.

Hector sits up, rubs his eyes.

We sit in silence, watching the television.

'Kylan called earlier,' Hector says. 'While you were out. He's coming for dinner tomorrow night.'

I feel myself breathe in sharply. 'He's coming home?'

'They're coming for dinner and the night,' he says. 'They have work on Monday.'

'Katya's coming too, then?' I ask.

'Of course,' he says. 'You can meet her at last. They have some news.'

'It's about time he brought her home,' I say. 'It almost feels like she doesn't exist.'

Hector watches me. 'Yes,' he says. 'It's a shame going to the city upsets you.'

I pause. 'It must be getting serious.'

'They live together,' Hector says. 'I'd say that's pretty serious.'

'But she hasn't met his mother,' I say.

Hector doesn't reply. We both look at the television screen.

'Did he want me to call him?' I say.

'He said there's no need.' I feel a sharp stab then, of being left out again. I remember the sounds of laughter from Hector's study, the gaps of contented thought, then the horrible click of the chess pieces.

'I'll go to the market in the morning, then,' I say.

'I'm sure we have enough food in the fridge,' Hector says.

I glance at him. 'I want to make halibut stew,' I say. 'It's Kylan's first time home in three months and I want to make his favourite.' It almost sounds like I am pleading.

I wait. Finally, Hector nods.

'I've invited my mother,' he says.

I sigh. 'But where is everyone going to sleep?' I ask.

'Put Kylan and Katya in the guest room and my mother in Kylan's room.'

'Kylan can't sleep in the guest room,' I say.

'Why not?'

'It's not his room.'

Hector half smiles. 'I doubt he'll mind.'

I mind.

'I better go and get the rooms ready,' I say, moving to get up.

'Can't you do that tomorrow?'

I sit back down.

Hector turns back to the television, his jaw tight. Out of the corner of my eye, I watch for the signs: the drooping eyelids, the slowing of his breathing. He is drifting off. When I am sure he is asleep, I leave the room.

I walk upstairs and along the corridor to Kylan's room. My watch says eight thirty. Through the crack in the door, I think I see his small body curled under the dinosaur duvet cover. Though the light still glows at the edges of the curtains, it's bedtime. On the chest of drawers a small golden trophy stands: one he recently won in a handball tournament at school. His sandy hair rests on the pillow and I step forward, longing to stroke it until he falls asleep. Then I see a younger Hector, leaning over the bed, and I take a step back.

'What's the matter, Kylan?' Hector is saying.

At first, Kylan doesn't answer, and I see his head shake on the pillow; he covers his face with his hands.

'What's up? You can tell me.'

Still nothing. Inwardly, I smile. Hector thinks he's so good at this.

'I won't tell your mother.'

Kylan lifts his head up from the pillow, takes his hands away from his face, and looks at his father. He speaks softly, but I still hear him.

'She won't tell me about them,' he says.

I remember, then, Kylan's upturned face with his father's blue eyes and the smattering of freckles. I was silent at first, pretending I hadn't heard him, but he kept pushing and pushing me, as he did when he wanted something from the supermarket. *Please, Mum, please, Mum, please, Mum.* I snapped and told him to shut up. I didn't want to lie to him, my son. He was silent then, staring out of the window at the green fields. His silence continued through teatime, and bedtime, and he refused to say good night to me when I came to tuck him in. I pleaded with him, my voice full of trapped tears, but he still didn't speak a word to me.

'She won't tell you about who?' Hector asks.

'She won't tell me about her mummy and daddy,' Kylan says.

Hector is silent.

'Everyone else at school has two sets,' he says. 'I only have Granny. It's not fair.'

I sigh. It can't be true that everyone has four grandparents.

'Mummy's parents are dead,' Hector says finally. 'They died when she was younger, before I met her. She doesn't like to talk about it because it makes her sad.'

Hector sits on the edge of the bed, his arm snaked over Kylan's side.

'How did they die?' Kylan asks.

'They were in a car accident,' he says. 'Don't ask Mummy about it any more. We don't want her to be upset.'

I rest my head against the wall, my eyes burning. I know I can't let myself think about that: it's somewhere I am not allowed to go.

Kylan is silent. Then he nods, sinking back down under the covers.

When I open the door, the room is empty and dim. Without turning the light on, I sit down on the edge of the bed. I don't come in here often. The walls are bare, and I know that in the wardrobe only a few misshapen hangers are left in the darkness. I lean back, turning over and burying my face into the duvet, breathing through the thickness of the material. Only the sweetness of fabric softener fills my nose. I long for the smell of baby Kylan's dim beige room: a harmless smell, of something familiar, like biscuits dipped in tea. His hands on the solid white bars of the cot; his feet sinking into the thin mattress; his legs stiff, defiant. His vertical blond hair, and his eyes watching for any movement. An excited smile, and then his face against the cotton of my shoulder as I carry him to the changing table. I know he can't remember these things, so I will have to, for both of us.

After he left in the summer, I would find my way here in the middle of the night. I would slide under the duvet and wake up crying, knowing he wasn't coming back. As he packed his room into boxes, I told him it would be best to leave some things here, that it was all too sudden, but he shrugged me off, excited about moving in with Katya and his new job at the bank. I wanted to tell him it was too soon: he didn't know her well enough. I thought he was being selfish. He couldn't see that if he moved to the city I would never see him. He knows I don't like the city: I haven't been there in twenty-five years. I wanted to shout at him, grab his arms, and tell him not to leave me.

But I had told him all that before, when he wanted to go to university in the city. I begged him to stay, to go to college locally. I told him he would break my heart. One night, we sat again at the kitchen table to discuss it, Hector and Kylan on one side, me on the other. My argument was that the local college was good, that he could get his qualifications and work at the farm up the road. Hector thought he should go to the city, live his own life. I have never forgiven him for that.

I started to cry then, slow deliberate tears. Kylan sat on the other side of the table and watched me for a long time. Hector sighed. I put my head in my hands, heard Kylan's chair scraping on the kitchen tiles, and felt him put his arms around me. *It's OK, Mum*, he whispered. *I'll stay.*

I smile to myself, a warmth moving through my chest. He's coming home. Tomorrow, Kylan will be here and everything will be all right again. I'll show him everything he has left behind. And I'll do it all without my pills. There's so much to do, I can barely wait to get started. I tell myself he won't leave me again.

I go to our bathroom and wash my face. Leaning close to the mirror, I see the lines around my eyes, the traces of grey in my hair. Smiling, I watch the furrows deepen. My skin is paler than most of the women in the valley, those who help out on the farms. My hands are paler too, less marked, though the undersides have hardened from all the cleaning products. My wedding ring is so much a part of my hand now, I don't see it any more. I never had an engagement ring: I suppose we were never really engaged.

In my bedroom, I pull on my woollen nightgown and slip beneath the covers. Touching my stomach, I push it out, imagining I am pregnant again. That feeling, of your body no longer being yours but the property of someone else, someone more important. I remember the sickness too. Before I knew I was pregnant, I thought there was something really wrong with me.

One day, on my way to the market, I had to pull the car over and vomit onto the grassy verge. I drove myself straight to the doctor's surgery on the other side of the water. Asking for an appointment, I felt ashamed, as if I was betraying Hector, by admitting there was something wrong in the new life he had worked so hard to build for us. I read the posters on the walls of the waiting room, my hands quivering against my green skirt, not making eye contact with anyone in case I knew them or they knew Hector.

The receptionist had to call my name three times before I recognized it. *Marta Bjornstad.* Blushing, I made my way along the draughty corridor.

'You're expecting a baby,' the doctor said once she had run her tests, looking up from behind a desk cluttered with paperclipped documents and family memorabilia.

I felt my mouth fall open. 'But I'm ill,' I said. 'I've been dreadfully sick.'

The doctor smiled, writing something. 'That's perfectly normal. I'm prescribing folic acid.'

'But I don't feel right,' I said.

She didn't look up. 'It's all worth it in the end,' she said. 'When the baby arrives.'

It felt so strange that something had been happening in my body which I was unaware of. I put my hands on my tummy but it didn't feel any different. As I walked out of the doctor's surgery into the sunshine, I smiled, imagining someone to talk to, to look after. I held onto the knowledge as if it was something precious. Hector could tell something was different: I hummed to myself making the dinner, smiling more than usual. I waited until we were in bed that night, sitting side by side, before I told him. He shifted his position, leaning over me and searching my face. Then he pulled me towards him into a hug, squeezing me gently, and I knew then that this was what he wanted, that he was as happy as I was.

Leaving the light on for Hector, I turn onto my side and shut my eyes.

6

In the middle of the night, I jerk awake, my eyes wet. The illuminated alarm clock by the side of the bed reads 02:13. Moonlight shines dimly through the crack in the curtains, and I can just make out a white disc in the night sky. A full moon.

I was dreaming of a forest. A figure was running, as fast as she could, the green of the trees rushing darkly past. I remember a flash of white-blonde hair, a shriek of laughter, her muscular limbs pushing forward. The ballet shoes she wore on her feet. Ribbons trailed behind her, skimming the dirt.

I breathe out. I am in my own bed, warm and safe. Hector is on my side, his arms around me. I imagine him, lying awake in the darkness, watching the outline of my body, working up the courage to move closer. I can feel his warm belly against my back; the looseness of the skin like silk; the flesh soft, harmless. I listen to the rise and fall of his breathing: the slight wheeze in his lungs, the rattle of his throat. I put my hands over his: the skin feels dry.

There is no sound in the room except for our breathing, my heartbeat in my chest. I feel a twisting anxiety begin in my stomach. I try to make myself calm, to go back to sleep, but the darkness is heavy, the silence oppressive. I long for the sound of the outside nighttime: an owl in the forest, a fox wailing.

When I can't bear it any more, I slip away from Hector and out of bed, pulling myself up. Walking towards the hallway, I wince at the creak of the hinges.

Away from the warm bedroom, the air is sharp. I long for my dressing gown, hanging on the other side of the door. Over the banisters of the staircase is one of Hector's ironed shirts and my black trousers, ready to be put away. I pull off my nightgown and slip them on. The shirt is made of thick wool and reminds me of Wellington boots, chopping wood, and the smell of pastry. Warm, wholesome things.

Shafts of moonlight trespass across the hallway, casting shadows behind the picture frames. I rub my finger over the light switch on the wall. I don't press it: Hector is sleeping, but I imagine the light spreading down the dark corridor. I am good at this. Soon, the black square of the window is white.

I walk to Kylan's bedroom, opening the cupboard doors to look for traces of him. At the back, I find a pair of balled-up socks and an old magazine about stamp collecting, yellowed at the edges. Holding the socks to my nose, I breathe them in, but there is nothing. Eventually, I put the things back where I found them.

Turning around, I see a girl, sitting on the floor with her back against the bed. I let out a gasp, but she doesn't seem to see me. She stares without blinking, her grey eyes wide and glossy. Her hair is very messy: dirty, almost grey, though the broken ends are blonde. She is wearing grimy white pyjamas, her thin arms wrapped loosely around her bony knees. The bed is different: low with a metal frame, and a thin foam mattress covered with a white sheet.

A strand of hair falls forward into her face. She doesn't notice; I long to reach forward and brush it out of her eyes. Then she looks straight up at me.

'Help me,' she says.

As I step towards her, she disappears. The bed is as it was. I go and stand in front of where she was sitting, lean down and look under the bed, but there is nothing there. I tell myself I must have imagined it. It isn't real, I say. But I can still hear the desperation in her voice, and see her huge grey eyes. I try to remember if this is what happened last time I stopped taking my pills, but I can't. The part of me that watches from the outside is intrigued. Something is happening at last.

I walk quickly back down the corridor, thinking with every step that I see something in the corner of my eye. In our bedroom, I pull back the covers and crawl into bed. It is so warm. I lean in to Hector, pulling his arms around me. I feel him stir.

'What's the matter?' he says sleepily.

'I couldn't sleep,' I say, drawing him even closer. 'I had a bad dream.'

I feel him wrap his body around mine. I think then of telling him what I saw, but I know he will ask me if I have been taking my pills.

'You're so cold,' he says, his breath warm on my neck.

'I'm sorry,' I say.

'Go back to sleep,' he says, and I shut my eyes.

Lying in the darkness, I hear his breaths slow, and I match mine with his.

*

I wake again at seven to the sound of the alarm. Hector is on his side of the bed and I am on mine.

He switches off the sound and I turn over, watching the blue edge of the curtains. It makes me think of the early days, before we were married, when I spent so much time in this bed. I wasn't well then: I could barely sit up, but waking in the night and seeing the orange summer light around the curtains made me feel a little better. I would lie awake, listening to Hector breathing, thinking of nothing but the light-filled valley above the dim bedroom, and listening to the alien sounds of birds in the trees. My fingers trembled under the duvet cover, stretching towards the window.

Hector was so good to me in those days. He took time off work, sat with me while we watched old movies, and wiped the tears from my cheeks. I was ill, grieving, and he took care of me, with food and cups of tea and hot-water bottles. He knew I didn't want to see anyone, so he kept me a secret, didn't force me to get up, to pull myself together. He made sure I took my medicine, and slowly I began to put on weight, to get better. I owe him so much.

I get out of bed, creeping towards the bedroom door so as not to wake Hector. He likes to sleep in on Saturdays, and I have a lot to do for this evening. He'll be down at about nine for his eggs, and I will have them ready.

Downstairs, I clear the mess in the living room: scooping up the newspaper, putting Hector's shoes into the hall cupboard, straightening the cushions, drawing the curtains.

Clear away any untidiness. Catering to his comfort will give you an immense sense of personal satisfaction.

Setting up the ironing board, I put on my *20 Romantic Classical Favourites* CD and work to the 'Moonlight Sonata'. Everything gets ironed, including Hector's underpants.

Find little jobs that will make his life easier and more pleasant.

Listening to the rise and swell of the music, the muscles in my legs begin to twitch, as if I have trapped a nerve. They long to be stretched. Putting the iron down, I place my hands face down on the ironing board. As I point my toes, my legs lengthen and the gentle hairs catch the light. The music reaches a crescendo and I pull my leg up further, ignoring a tremor of pain.

Letting go, I move the ironing board and rise up onto the tips of my toes in one motion, feeling the arch of my foot. Stepping from one foot to the other, I lift my curved arms backwards and then forwards. My body knows what to do. I rise onto one leg, sweeping the other in a semicircle, raising my arms and turning, turning, turning, always bringing my head back to the same point.

Just as I am beginning to overbalance, I feel a hand

catch my leg and hold it, helping take the weight. There is another hand on the small of my back. I open my eyes and the girl from last night is there, smiling, swaying a little to the music as she supports me, her eyes closed.

I stay very still, not wanting her to go. Her blonde hair isn't as messy, tied up high on her head. The white pyjamas she was wearing the last time I saw her are clean now, too short at the arms and legs, dotted with tiny pink hearts. Her body is more filled out, and I can see the muscles of her legs, and the definition of her stomach. She opens her eyes and looks right at me.

'What are you doing?'

I jump, and turn towards the living-room door. Hector is standing there, watching me. I feel my cheeks redden. When I look behind me, she is gone.

'I didn't think you were up yet,' I say, my heart pounding.

A smile cracks the corner of Hector's mouth. 'You look ridiculous,' he says. 'What was that supposed to be?'

I look down at the floor.

He laughs then, short and sharp. 'You looked like a crazy person. Dancing in your nightgown. Whatever next? Just wait until I tell Kylan.'

I shoot him a look. 'Don't, Hector,' I say. 'Please.'

He smiles. 'I won't,' he says, moving closer, putting his hand on my back where hers was a moment ago. 'Not if you don't want me to.' He rubs my back, up and down. 'Have you taken your pill?' he says.

'Not yet,' I say.

Hector leaves the room, returning with the bottle.

'Open your mouth,' he says.

He takes out a pink pill and puts it in my mouth. I mock-swallow, letting the pill slip underneath my tongue, then open again. He nods.

Once he has left, I spit the pill into my hand, going to the fireplace and dropping it into the grate. Then I move the ironing board back into place and continue to work.

There is something, just out of reach, which I can feel shifting inside me. I shut my eyes, willing it to come forward. It's a smell first, of detergent and sweat, and a rapid image that shuttles before my eyes too fast for me to grasp. Hard, shiny wood floors, a wall lined with mirrors. The tight material against my legs, my hair scraped back and held aloft with too many sharp pins. Then the chords: classical music played softly, a few bars and then nothing. The picture spreads for a moment like ink through blotting paper, and then, just as quickly, it is gone.

After what feels like a long time, Hector re-enters the

room. He walks slowly to his chair, easing himself into it. I hear the newspaper open. The only sound is the rustle of the pages and the hiss of the iron. The palm of my hand is slippery with sweat, making it hard to get a good grip.

Some time later, when I am finished, I turn to lift the pile of ironed clothes into the basket, and catch a glimpse of him. He holds the newspaper up, but he is staring straight past it, at the far wall. He looks so tired and old and drawn, his half-moon spectacles resting on his nose. His face is clouded with something I can't read. I almost don't recognize him.

I stand by the ironing board and watch as he lets the newspaper crumple in his lap, dropping his head into his hands. The iron hisses.

He lifts his head and looks at me. I can barely stand it. He is expecting something. I should know what to do.

Comfort him in times of stress. Speak in a low, soft voice to reassure him of your support.

'Hector?' I say. 'Do you want some eggs?'

He gets up, lifting himself out of the chair. Standing behind me, he puts his arms around my waist, resting his neck onto my shoulder.

'We've been happy together, haven't we?' he asks.

I nod, my hair brushing against his cheek.

'Don't ever leave me,' he says softly.

'I won't,' I say.

'Tell me you love me,' he says.

'I love you, Hector,' I say.

He turns me around, pulling me towards him and kissing me on the mouth, his eyes still open.

He releases me, then he smiles and walks towards the door. There's the sound of the front door slamming, and the car starting up in the drive.

7

Hector leaves the house at eight thirty. After getting dressed in some old clothes, I fetch the duster and cleaning spray from under the sink and return to the living room. Starting at the bay window, I wipe down everything, making sure not to miss a spot.

I reach Hector's chess set, in pride of place on the table in the centre of the room. Sitting on the floor, I rub one piece at a time, turning to look out of the window as I work. Behind me, I hear the sound of a marble chess piece sliding across the board. I turn and see her sitting cross-legged on the floor, her legs so thin that the gaps between them are vast. Her hand is still on a white pawn, which she has pushed forward two spaces.

I look at her face: the dirty, narrow cheeks; the matted hair; her glowing grey eyes. She smiles as I slide a black pawn forward to meet hers, her white teeth too large in her head. She takes her turn, her legs jigging in the white pyjamas.

As I am wondering what has happened since the last time I saw her, I feel her hand over mine. Looking down at our two hands together, I see both sets of fingernails are bitten to the quick, raw at the edges. I put my other hand on top of hers, and suddenly, her hand is gone and the room is empty.

The pieces on the chess board are paused, mid-game. I wonder if that proves that she was really here. It felt real: I can still feel her cold hand over mine. I imagine telling Hector about it, and I see his face falling, then hear the rattle of the pill bottle.

I think of the house, of Kylan coming home, and I want to make him proud of me. I don't want to disappoint them again.

One after another, I move from room to room, cleaning everything in sight, until the whole house shines. I don't stop to look around or to check my progress. A few times, I remember the hidden cigarettes under the mattress, but I am not tempted to take a break. It feels good to be busy, to be working hard, and I barely think about Hector or what he is doing out for so long. It is like the old days, when Kylan was young, and I never had a moment to myself. It's not until I am wiping down the final stretch of kitchen surface that I look up at the window in the kitchen and realize the light is fading already, that the day is nearly gone. It's four p.m.

I pour myself a glass of wine and go to stand by the patio doors. I feel better, more like myself. Looking out at the garden, I see the dark line of the trees on the horizon, lit from behind by the pure blue of the failing sky. Kylan and Katya will be getting ready to leave, preparing themselves for the long drive from the city, through the shadows to the warm light of the house. I feel my excitement and hold on to it: Kylan is coming home.

As I stand at the sink, washing out the cleaning cloth again, I hear the sound of footsteps running across the landing upstairs. Walking out into the hallway, I catch the sound of laughter.

'Hello?' I call. I climb the stairs slowly. I hear a door closing and hurry up the last few stairs. Everything is still. The only door closed is that of Hector's study and I find myself opening it. We have an unwritten rule that I don't come in here, that this is Hector's place.

The big black tree outside the window blocks the light. Flicking the light on, the room is empty. I see sheets of unordered paper; strange lists of symbols, numbers and equals signs, with Hector's red marks in the margins; piles of journals; the sheaves of an old newspaper. There is a coffee ring on the faux mahogany which I trace with my fingers, and a nearby mug, still half full, with a thick white scum forming on the surface.

The notice board glares down at me from the far wall, studded with colourful postcards from old students neatly lined up, held on tight with a drawing pin in each corner. It has been here since I moved into the house: one of the first things Hector showed me. They were important to him, these young women, and the cards they sent were a sign that he was important to them too. I sensed that whatever it was they gave him was something I was now expected to provide.

I walk over to it, reach up and unpin a postcard: a black-and-white print of a girl sitting in a cafe, a cigarette in her hand. Turning the card over, I see slanted blue writing. *Thanks for all your help . . . I wouldn't be here without you.* I place it back on the board, being careful to line it up with the others. I turn over another, a blue Matisse woman. Different writing on the back. *Interview went well . . . lucky we went over differential equations!* When I see the kisses on the end of this one, I pull it off the board and let it go, watching it drop towards the ground.

Underneath, there is a photograph I recognize. My younger face smiles out at me, looking straight into the camera. My hair is short and dark, level with my chin, and I have a dark fringe which almost covers my wide grey eyes. I can see the buds of new life on the bare trees in the background, and the valley rising behind me.

I have seen this picture before, many times, and I remember the story of it. Hector has always said it was a Saturday morning. We had followed our usual routine: Hector slept in while I fried his eggs and bacon. I had spinach and one poached egg. I remember that the pregnancy demanded a strict diet, which Hector had written out and stuck on the fridge for me. We wanted to give Kylan the best possible chance of being healthy and strong. We had discussed it, and I understood, taking a huge amount of satisfaction from having a new, important reason to take care of myself, of my body. As usual, we took our walk around the valley at exactly ten o'clock.

Before, when I have seen this picture and listened to Hector's words, I could picture the valley in a general way: the leaves, the green fields. Hector told me that we walked arm in arm, and so I saw us doing that. I can't usually remember any smells or feelings, but as I look at the photograph now, I remember a particular day, the one this photograph was taken. I can hear the birdsong and the sound of gravel underfoot. Hector had brought his camera, an old Nikon, and took pictures of the beginnings of spring. The crisp, clean light made every-thing feel untouched. There were orange crocuses bursting through the sterile brown earth; the trees were punctuated with green. Hector took my picture as I put my hand out to touch the new leaves emerging from dark bark. I looked at him, surprised, and he smiled.

We always followed the same route, but that day, I felt odd, my usual energy slipping away as I watched Hector's walking boots march on and on. Looking upwards at the stretches of green and the blue sky beyond them, I had vertigo, as if I was standing on top of the mountains looking down, rather than the other way around. My knees buckled and Hector caught me, his strong hands grasping my arms.

'It's all right,' he said. 'You're safe.'

He led me over to a bench by the side of the road, and we sat down.

'What's the matter?' he said. 'Is everything all right?'

As I caught my breath, I looked up at him, his brow furrowed. He put his hands out and touched my stretching stomach.

'We shouldn't have come out today,' he said. 'Shall I go and get help?'

I shook my head. 'I'm fine,' I said. 'I just felt a bit dizzy, but I'm OK now.'

Hector looked at me sternly. 'You should be more careful,' he said. 'If you feel ill, please tell me. It's important.'

I looked down at his hands, still on my stomach.

His face changed then, a smile spreading. 'I just want what's best for the baby,' he said.

Just then, I felt Kylan moving in my stomach, shifting against Hector's hands. 'I love it when he does that,' he said, 'it's as if he's telling us that he's here, waiting for us.'

I put my hands over Hector's, surprised to see a tear forming in his eye.

'I'm so happy,' he said. 'We're going to be a family. It's what I've always wanted.'

'I'm happy too,' I said, touching my proud belly.

'Mother was so worried I wouldn't find a wife,' he said. 'She was always saying I'd left it too late, worrying about who would take care of me when she was gone. I heard her talking to my father once, wondering if there was something wrong with me. But then I found you. It hasn't been easy, but it's all worth it now.'

He kissed me. As I waited for him to pull away, Kylan shifted again. Then we got up and walked back towards the house, our home, Hector supporting me with one arm.

Back in the study, I can feel one of my headaches starting. I rub at my temples, but the pain is spreading already and there will soon be little I can do. I feel something, then, pressing against my back. It's her, I can smell her breath, feel it on the back of my neck. I long to turn around, but I am afraid she will disappear again. I feel her thin body against mine, her breath warm, close to my ear now. She whispers something that I can barely make out.

'Marta?'

Hector is standing next to me, his hand on my arm, the fingernails long, the thick skin crisscrossed with lines. The sharp smell of fish is in the room, and I see the bag in his other hand, thick with something solid. The halibut. He has been to the market for me.

'You got the fish,' I say.

His hand is still on my skin. As he stares at me, he begins to tighten his grip, slowly, almost as if he doesn't realize he is doing it.

'Hector,' I say, 'you're hurting me.'

He lets go. 'What are you doing in here?' he says.

I look at the notice board, at the photo, then at the floor where the discarded postcard lies. 'I was cleaning,' I say.

He follows my gaze, and bending down awkwardly to pick up the postcard, he slots it back into its place, covering up the photograph again.

I reach out for the halibut and he passes it to me, still staring at the notice board. He shifts the postcard slightly so it lines up with the others. Then he looks at me, and something hangs in the air between us, something thick and dark like smoke. Standing here, I am finding it hard to breathe.

'Hector?' I say.

He doesn't answer.

'Are you all right?'

He nods. I wonder, then, if he has been seeing things too.

'Hector,' I say, 'I want to talk to you about something. Have you noticed anything odd in the house? I've been hearing things.'

'What kind of things?' he asks.

'I don't know – noises. My doll was turned the other way yesterday.'

Hector smiles. 'Is your imagination playing tricks again?' he says.

'I don't think I'm imagining it, Hector.'

'I'd have thought you'd have grown out of this by now: making up stories.'

'But I'm seeing things too,' I say. 'A blonde girl.'

Hector's eyebrows rise. 'Have you been taking your pills?'

I swallow. 'You know I have, Hector.'

He takes my wrist again. 'If I find out you've been missing them again—' He stops. He pinches the flesh at my waist. 'You're losing weight,' he says. 'Have you eaten today?'

'I haven't had time,' I say. 'There's been so much to do.'

Always put the needs of the rest of the family above your own.

'Eat something before they get here,' he says. 'Is everything ready?'

'Almost,' I say.

'Do you need any help?'

Never bother your husband with domestic matters.

I shake my head. 'I just need to make the halibut stew.'

Hector looks at his watch. 'I'll go and get ready then,' he says, turning around and leaving the room.

*

Some time later, after I have finished in the kitchen, I listen in the hallway for signs of Hector. After a few minutes, the floor creaks and I know he is in his study.

I climb the stairs. In the bathroom, the fan whirrs. I shut and lock the door, turning on the shower, watching the water begin to flow, turning the air to steam. Removing my clothes, I feel disgusting, itchy with accumulated dirt, and I long to be clean again. In the mirror, my collar bones rise through the white skin, my breasts suspended, small and flat, from my chest. The sagging skin of my stomach is loose and wrinkled.

The water runs hot, and already the edges of the glass have begun to steam up. It's excruciating, but I make myself bear it. My hair dampens and clings to the back of my neck. I lather the soap between my palms and wash my body slowly, making sure not to miss an inch of skin. When I am clean, I close my eyes and focus on the darkness behind my lids, the hot wet flow of the water on my chest. I stand there as long as I can.

When I open my eyes, I'm outside the shower cubicle, looking in. I can hear the rush of water, and through the misted glass I make out the girl's silhouette. She is singing to herself: no words, just a hummed tune, vibrating under the water and through the echoey bathroom. I peer through small clear circles in the glass. She has her eyes shut, but she's smiling, her skin white and smooth under the bathroom lights. Her blonde hair has darkened, slicked back, moulding itself smoothly to the shape of her curved shoulders and back. Her hips jut out from her waist and her ribs protrude from her chest. She has no breasts. I can see the thick blue veins beneath her white skin, and there are fine hairs all over her body.

Her eyes snap open, clear and grey, and I step backwards, out of sight. The humming has stopped now, and I listen, trying to hear her again. But there is only the sound of the water drumming into the empty base, and when I step forward, her pink silhouette is gone.

I reach back into the cubicle and switch off the water, looking around me at the duck-egg blue of the tiles, Hector's shaving things by the sink, his robe on the back of the door. I am shivering; my teeth chattering, and I pull a towel from the rail and rub myself with it, hard. I stand there for some time, watching the empty shower cubicle, tracing my wet footprints across the carpet.

Looking over my shoulder, I see myself in the steamed mirror. I don't want to push the girl away, to deny these things I have been seeing. There's a sense that it would be fruitless anyway: like trying to sink a cork in basin full of water. It will always rise to the surface again.

*

In the bedroom, I go to the wardrobe. I am careful about choosing what I want to wear, running my finger along the selection of clothes. Tonight feels important and I want to look my best.

A good woman can be judged by the neatness of her dress and how well her children behave.

I want Kylan to be proud of me.

I choose a red pencil skirt with a matching jacket and a white shirt. Perhaps I will wear heels too.

At the back of the wardrobe, I catch a glimpse of crumpled white material. I reach in and touch it, the lace edge slipping through my fingers. I haven't thought about this in years. Pulling it out, I decide to wear it tonight, my secret. A corset: a wedding gift from Hector. When I used to wear it, it was fastened on the tightest clasp, but these days even the loosest is too tight, and I struggle to turn the material around my middle. When it is on, I can feel the slight bulges of skin along the edges of the wired material: I feel restricted, but I decide that it is not altogether a bad thing.

I remember trying the corset on in the changing room of a department store, on our last trip to the city. We had been shopping all day, for clothes for my new married life, a special treat. We agreed it was a good day, wandering around the sunlit city, stopping for a coffee in one of the wide tree-lined avenues. I remember Hector smiling, wiping away a trail of white foam from his lip. It wasn't long before the wedding and it was summer.

Now though, I am taken back to the stuffy smell of the changing room. My hands shook as I attached the clasps and I had to ask Hector to help me with the top few. I remember how cold his hands felt. I adjusted it behind the curtain, slipping my arms through the straps, but though the material sagged, it was suddenly too tight, and I couldn't breathe. I pulled at it, my face hot, but it wouldn't come off. Eventually I got myself out of it, and pulled on my clothes: an old jumper of Hector's and some black trousers, too big. For a long time, I wouldn't come out of the changing room, and Hector had to persuade me, first with kind words and encouragements, then quiet threats, whispered through the thick velvet curtain which divided us. *Would your daughter like some help?* the changing-room attendant asked, and even through the curtain, I could feel Hector's quiet rage.

After we had paid, Hector took me by the arm and we walked through the streets. I couldn't keep up with him, and I remember how his grip tightened. I wanted to do the right thing, but everything I did seemed to annoy him, and his eyes were dark, his lips tight. He muttered at me to hurry up. Eventually, we came to a hairdresser's salon and Hector pulled me inside.

I can smell the alcohol of the salon again now. I breathe in: just beyond it, there are other things, and I wait. There is the feel of the leather seat under my fingers, the huge mirrors in front of me. In the reflection, I see myself, but I look different, almost unrecognizable.

I remember the hairdresser asking me when I had last

had it cut, her voice filled with thinly veiled disgust as she held the ends up to the light. I shook my head, feeling the eyes of the other people in the shop. The music, the laughter, the chatter, all existed beyond an impassable wall. Hector sat by the window affecting boredom, casting glances across at me, a magazine juddering on his knee. He had tried so hard to get the knots out, even suggesting he cut my hair himself. The tears rolled down my cheeks. I could feel his embarrassment as the hairdresser knelt down beside me, her own hair gleaming under the lights, and whispered that it would all be all right.

She gave me a hot sweet cup of tea, which I drank quickly to make her happy, burning my tongue. Then, according to Hector's instructions, she cut it all off, gave me a fringe, and dyed it brown. Watching the ground and the long wisps that fell, I listened to the determined metallic sound of the scissors.

When she switched off the blow-dryer, I let myself look. My head felt lighter, and although I didn't recognize the girl in the mirror with the dark bob and heavy fringe, I knew it was me. Hector put down his magazine and came over, smiling widely. He thanked the hairdresser, then bent down to me.

'Do you like it, Marta?' he asked.

I nodded.

'It must be a relief to get rid of all that hair,' he said. 'You look like a different person.'

He turned around, walking to the till, and I watched the girl with the dark hair get up and follow him.

For all these years, I have thought of that day in the city as one full of light and joy. Hector and I, beginning our lives together. Now it's as if I can see shadows for the first time.

8

Once I am ready, I go to the kitchen and drink two glasses of white wine as quickly as I can. I wash the glass, dry it and put it back into the cupboard. Hector definitely wouldn't approve, not with his mother arriving any second.

At exactly seven thirty, I sit and wait at the top of the stairs. Soon, I hear a car. The headlights beam mistily through the frosted-glass panel in the front door, the car doors open and shut, and there is laughter and clipping heels in the driveway.

When I hear the doorbell, I stand up, moving slowly, methodically, in my high heels. Holding the handrail with one hand, I feel lightheaded. Steadying myself at the bottom, I glance in the hall mirror, smile, and feel a rush of happiness. Behind the glass across the hallway is the outline of my son's broad shoulders, his hair darkened in silhouette.

I open the door, letting the chill of the outside air in.

He is standing on the doorstep, his hands in the pockets of a big grey duffle coat I don't recognize, wearing the red scarf I gave him for Christmas. He still looks like a boy to me, his sandy-brown hair split down the centre, his freckled cheeks, and his kind blue eyes.

I say his name. He leans in to kiss me on the cheek and there's the sharp tang of his aftershave, covering up his smell. Pulling him closer, his body feels strange, big, not how I remember.

Over his shoulder, the blonde girl is standing on the mat, smiling a crooked half-smile at me, wearing her white pyjamas with the pink hearts. I breathe in sharply, clutching Kylan's arms, the material of his coat thick under my fingers. He puts his hands over mine, gently, trying to lift them off. My heart moves heavily. He holds me at arm's length, looking at me with darting eyes.

'What's the matter?' he says.

I take a step backwards, into the hallway. Kylan enters, and she starts to follow him. Pushing past Kylan towards the door, I shut it quickly. I hear her make a noise from the other side. I turn to face Kylan, my breath rising quickly, standing between him and her.

'Mum,' he says. 'What the hell is going on?'

'She can't come in here,' I say.

'She's come to meet you. We've just driven for six hours—'

'That's not her.'

'You've never met her.'

'She can't come in.'

Kylan goes to open the door. I stand in his way.

'Mum,' he says, 'please. It's freezing out there.'

His blue eyes are so like his father's. Walking around him, I go to the kitchen. I hear Kylan open the door, then shut it; I hear them talking. *I don't know. I'm sorry.*

Now, Hector is on the stairs. Out of sight, I see his hair is still a little wet from the shower, brushed across his head neatly, like a little boy dressed up uncomfortably for a birthday party. He goes to give her a kiss on the cheek. She colours, and there is an awkward moment when they almost bump noses. She has the same blonde hair, long over her shoulders, the same pale grey eyes, but a different mouth. Her lips are smaller, like a rosebud; her smile is slower, softer. She is wearing a pretty flowered dress. It's not the girl after all.

I step forward.

They all turn to look at me. There is a long moment where no one speaks.

'Mother not here yet?' Hector says.

I don't answer. Hector looks between us.

'Have you met Katya at last?' he says.

'No,' I say.

Hector looks confused. 'Who let them in, then?'

'I'm sorry, Katya,' I say, stepping forward. 'I didn't know you were coming.'

Both Hector and Kylan stare at me. 'But I told you—' Hector says.

'I'm sure we will have enough food to go around,' I say, smiling.

'It's lovely to meet you at last, Mrs Bjornstad,' Katya says finally. 'I've heard so much about you.'

I wonder what she has heard.

'You can call her Marta,' Hector says.

I stare at her. Her pretty, unblemished face shines back at me. Watching Kylan's arm move around her back, pulling her closer towards him, I feel something cold shifting in my stomach.

'Can I get anyone a drink?' I say, taking a step towards the kitchen.

'I can get them—' Hector says.

'Take them through to the living room, Hector. The fire's lit.'

They stare at me and no one answers. I feel like I am about to scream.

'I'll have a beer,' Hector says.

'Me too,' Kylan says.

'Do you have gin and tonic?' Katya asks.

'I have your favourite beer,' I say, looking only at Kylan. 'I bought it specially.' He looks down at his feet.

In the kitchen, I put my hands on the edge of the counter and listen until they are out of the hall. They don't move. Through the crack in the kitchen door, over the echoes of my breathing and heartbeat, I hear them.

Once I am sure they are gone, shuffling through to the living room, I lean over and vomit quickly into the sink. A slithering trail of brown runs across the stainless steel. Behind my eyelids, there's the pressure of a dim bedroom: Kylan's little hand on my shoulder, the crease between his wide eyes. The same look of concentration and worry, familiar from hours of maths homework. I remember his football kit, his muddy knees, the smell of the wet hairs at the nape of his neck.

Turning on the tap, I rub at the mess until it is clean again. Then I wipe and rinse my mouth, wash my hands, and take one tumbler, two tankards, and a wine glass out of the cupboard.

I slop gin and tonic water into the tumbler without measuring them. Cutting a lemon with unsteady hands, I see the knife glint under the kitchen light. I hold it in my hand for a moment; I feel an itch on my wrist, along the slender bone on the underside where the blue veins run. I go to rub the feeling away with the blade of the knife: as soon as the metal touches my skin, it clatters onto the sideboard.

They stop talking for a narrow moment as I enter the living room, then continue with false normality. I am aware of being watched as I hand the drinks out, leaving Kylan's until last. Katya says thank you. When I give Kylan his, he takes the glass without looking at me, his hand still resting on Katya's back.

The doorbell rings. Hector's mother stands on the doorstep. She seems smaller than I remember, older: the lines on her face coated with powder, accentuating the fine hairs on her cheeks. She wears an old blue suit which I recognize, and matching blue eye shadow. She steps forward, handing me a bunch of yellow carnations wrapped in tight cellophane.

'These are for you,' she says. 'Brighten the place up a bit.'

'Thank you, Matilda,' I say, standing back to let her in. 'Can I take your jacket?'

She ignores me, looking around the room. This house is still her territory.

She starts to take off her jacket, watching me with her

cloudy blue eyes. I turn away first, hanging her coat over the stairs.

'Where's Hector?' she asks.

'He's in the living room with Kylan and his girlfriend,' I say.

She walks slowly across the hallway, her hip obviously making her uncomfortable. I don't help her.

'Kylan,' she says, reaching the door. 'Come and give your old grandmother a kiss.' Tufts of white hair surround her head like a halo. Kylan bends to kiss her: she brushes his cheekbone leaving a trail of shimmering pink.

Matilda looks across at Katya.

'This is my girlfriend, Katya,' Kylan says.

Matilda scans her. 'It's lovely to meet you at last,' she says. 'Hector has told me a lot about you.'

'You too,' Katya says. I want to warn her.

Hector kisses his mother, and has his hair fussily smoothed. 'Let's have a look at you, Hector,' Matilda says, holding him at arm's length. She frowns. 'You look as if you need feeding up.' She looks at me, and I pretend not to notice, though my skin crawls.

'Can I get you a drink?' I ask.

She turns to Hector, smiling sweetly. 'I'd love a gin and tonic.'

'Of course, Mother,' Hector says, moving towards the living-room door.

I intercept him. 'I'll get it.'

'I don't mind—'

'I'll get it, Hector,' I say. 'I need to put these in some water.' I lift the flowers in my hands, watching a yellow petal fall towards the ground.

Hector turns back and joins the circle behind me. I stand on the outside for a moment, trying to catch Kylan's eye. He is laughing at something his father is saying, and as he laughs, he tenses his arm around Katya, pulling her closer. I watch the taut muscles in his upper arm. Katya flicks her hair out of her eyes, and I feel a searing ache spread through my body as I watch her smile up at him.

In the kitchen, I take some scissors and cut the cellophane away from the flowers. I breathe out, separating them onto the worktop, touching the edges of the snipped stems. Filling a bucket with water, I drop the flowers in and open the patio doors, putting them outside where they belong. They will only die faster in the house.

I check on the food, skirting the edge of the soup pan with a wooden spoon, smiling at its perfect consistency. I make another gin and tonic.

When I look up, Matilda is there, standing in the

doorway, her wrinkled hands on her wide hips. I turn to face her.

'Can I get you anything?' I ask.

She takes two steps into the room.

'Do you need any help?' she asks.

Automatically, I step back, out of her way.

'I'm all right,' I say. 'Everything's pretty much ready.'

She reaches out to lift up the lid of the stew pot. Steam escapes into the kitchen, and she sniffs the air. Then she picks up the spoon from the side of the stove, ladles out some of the sauce, and sips it. She shuts her eyes, letting the hot liquid travel down her throat.

As I watch her, I remember a younger Matilda, full-bodied and wearing a red apron matching mine. After the wedding, she would come every Sunday, for my lessons. It almost makes me laugh that I ever thought I stood a chance of meeting her expectations. I was taking a job she didn't want to give up, especially since Hector's father had passed away. Despite the fact she had pressured Hector into finding a wife, she wasn't going to make it easy to take over from her. Hector would sit at the kitchen table, watching us. He was always annoyed with me after she left, barely speaking to me for the rest of the afternoon. I had disappointed him by failing to impress her, as he had failed before me.

Now, Matilda is still standing with her eyes closed, tasting my stew.

'Needs more salt,' she says. Then she turns around, picks up her gin and tonic from the sideboard, and leaves the room.

When she is gone, I lift the lid of the pan. Picking up the large salt container, I hold it over the stew, watching the smooth white trail disappear. I pour until the container is empty.

I run yet another bowl of soapy water at the sink, watching the steam rise. When the bowl is full, I turn off the taps, and plunge my hands below the surface, the heat tingling at the tips of my raw fingernails. I feel her hands slipping over mine, clasping my fingers, rubbing them. My eyes shut, her breath is hot in my ear, her weight presses against my back, and I can feel her bare feet on either side of mine. I wonder absently when I took off my shoes. She whispers something I can't make out. I strain to hear her.

When I take my hands out of the water, sweat breaks through the skin on my forehead, my hands shake, and she is gone.

9

In the living room, Hector is talking about the snow-fall last winter, telling the story again of how we were snowed in all over Christmas. Kylan is laughing along with him. I remember how keen he was to return to college as soon as the festivities were over: the snow frustrated his journey. He had to stay in the house for days, playing chess with his father and watching the fire burn away. He was irritable, forever checking the weather forecast. I suppose he must have forgotten.

'My parents have invited Kylan to stay for Christmas this year,' Katya says, glancing at Kylan. She glows in the light from the fireplace, her hair a shimmering mass of white gold. I clench my fists at my side. As she smiles, it is the other girl I see, smiling up at Kylan, talking to Hector. She is here, in this room, and I am the only one who can see her.

When I look around, I realize I'm in the centre of a silence. All of the faces in the circle are looking at me, waiting for my reaction to something, but I can't think what it was. I try to smile.

'Mum?' Kylan says.

I turn to him. 'Yes, darling?'

The line appears on his forehead again. 'I just asked you what we're going to eat.'

'I've made your favourite,' I say.

'Meatballs?' Katya says.

I stare at her, standing where the girl was. She flicks her blonde hair out of her eyes, blinks at me. 'No,' I say, my teeth gritted together, 'that's not Kylan's favourite. It's halibut stew.'

Kylan looks at the fire. 'I guess it depends what mood I'm in,' he says.

Hector laughs. It's loud, in the small room. 'Well handled, my boy,' he says, winking at Katya and making her blush.

'Did you just say you were spending Christmas with Katya's family?' I ask Kylan.

'We haven't decided yet,' he says.

'What about your father and me?' I say.

'They've only just invited us, so we haven't had a chance to think about it yet,' Kylan says.

'It's fine if you want to go there this year,' Hector says. 'We'll only be having the usual quiet Christmas.'

I think of the roast turkey and all the trimmings that take me days of preparation. Easy for him to say it will be quiet. I imagine Christmas dinner with Hector and his mother and I want to beg Kylan to come back.

Katya leans forward to pick up her glass and that's when I see it, on her left hand, a small square diamond on a silver band. Before I know what I'm doing, I have reached across and her hand is in mine.

'Where did you get this?' I ask.

Katya pauses. 'Kylan gave it to me.'

There is a long, long silence.

'Is this—' I say, looking at Kylan.

'I've asked Katya to marry me,' he says. 'That's what we wanted to tell you.'

The old look of concern is on his face again. I can feel her looking at me, all of them looking. My eyes begin to itch; my throat aches.

I hug him, pressing my face into his shoulder. 'That's such wonderful news,' I say, into his ear. 'I'm so happy for you.'

I pull back. I can see Katya is hiding a secret smile, of genuine happiness.

'Mum,' Kylan says, 'are you all right?'

The tears are beginning to spot my shirt. 'It's just such wonderful news, darling.'

I feel the tears begin to come faster.

'Let's get some champagne,' Hector says, and we leave the room together.

When we cross the threshold into the kitchen, I stop, feeling his hands on my shoulders. He turns me around and without looking up I bury my face in his chest. I feel him pull the door to behind us as I sob into him, and he puts his arms around me, holding me.

'He'll still come back, Marta,' he says. 'He just won't be living here any more.'

I look up at his calm blue eyes. 'But I miss him,' I say.

Hector strokes my hair. 'It had to happen eventually,' he says. 'We don't want him here for ever.'

I put my head back against his chest. *I do.*

'Why didn't he tell me?' I say softly.

Hector looks away, and I know then that Kylan had already told him. I imagine the phone conversation, Hector sitting behind the desk of his study, dishing out advice as if he is the expert on how to find a good wife.

'You knew?' I ask.

He rubs my back with his hand. 'I wanted to tell you,' Hector says, his voice soft, 'but he wasn't sure then. He asked me not to.'

I push him away.

'He shouldn't have asked her at all if he wasn't sure,'

I say. I pull out a chair and drag it over to the oven so that I can reach the wine rack above it. My heels sink as I lift myself up, denting the plastic covering. Unbalanced, I stand on the chair. I grasp the wall, feeling Hector watching me. He doesn't try to stop me.

Managing to grab a bottle of champagne, I tumble backwards, finding myself bundled in Hector's grasp.

'Marta, will you please be careful,' he says. 'I don't want you to hurt yourself.'

I extricate myself from him, putting the champagne bottle down onto the side, and walking out of the room. He can sort out the drinks.

*

I stop in the hallway, shutting my eyes and listening to the murmured rumblings of Kylan's voice through the closed door ahead. Pressing my head against the coolness of the paint, I try to steady myself. I'm not ready to go in there yet.

The voices have stopped. There is something on the other side of the door. I can smell the air coming from under it. Images begin to swim. A metal frame. One thin mattress: a neatly made bed. The creaking of springs.

The bedclothes are smooth and white and clean, and she is underneath them, tightly tucked in. She's wearing a pair of clean white pyjamas with small pink hearts all over them, brand new. They are not hers: too small, a child's size, tight across her chest, too short at the ankles.

There is a buzzing in the room like an insect caught, coming from the electric strip light which runs across the grey concrete ceiling, flickering slightly. A whirring too, ongoing, coming from a fan like the one in our bathroom, to keep the room from steaming up.

The room is square, with thick concrete walls. Against the opposite wall is a low white table, the paint bloated as if it has been outside in the rain. There is probably room to lie down lengthways between the bed and the table, but only just. There is a chair next to the bed, and in the corner there's a toilet without a lid, plumbed into the wall. Everything is nailed to the floor.

In the ceiling, there is a square metal door, with a sturdy looking padlock hanging from it.

A man is sitting on the edge of the bed, turned away from me. He sits and stares at her as she lies sleeping. I watch her eyes begin to open, slowly, as if it's painful. She tries to lift her head, to sit up, but she brings a hand up to her face, shuts her eyes tightly, and falls back again.

'Look at me,' he says. His voice is calm, and she begins to raise her eyes to his.

My eyes meet Kylan's. 'Mum, look at me,' he says. 'Are you all right?' He speaks softly.

I blink. 'I'm fine, darling,' I say.

He stares at me.

'Shall we go in?' I say.

He stands there for a moment. Behind him, I can see Matilda sitting in one of the armchairs; Katya on the sofa. Katya quickly looks away from me as I take in the room, but Matilda stares for longer than feels comfortable. I wipe under my eyes again. Kylan steps aside and I walk past him, taking a seat in Hector's armchair. I sit quietly, feeling my legs judder against the ground, trying to ignore my pressing headache. I want to see the room again, but the image is gone now and I can't bring it back.

There is a long, still silence: all that can be heard is the sound of wet wood cracking in the fireplace, and the agonizing tick of the clock over the mantelpiece. Matilda is staring at the blank television screen, her mouth a tight line.

Kylan reaches his arm along the cream sofa and Katya slides into the space he has made. Their movements are automatic, natural, as if sitting like that, their bodies touching, is the way they have always been. I wait for the conversation to pick up again. Katya puts her hand on Kylan's knee. He covers her hand with his, squeezing her fingers. I feel myself breathe in, and then I am at the living-room door, halfway up the stairs. It's too hard to be in that room any longer. The cold shifting thing in my stomach has been replaced by something sharp, as if something jagged has lodged itself deep in my flesh, too far in to get at.

10

In the dark bedroom, I crouch down by the bed, running my fingers underneath the mattress until I feel the two cigarettes, waiting side by side. I slide them out, rolling them into the palm of my hand.

My head sings as I stand up, and I shut my eyes against the glaring pressure. When I open them, her bare feet are there on the grey carpet, the dirty toenails almost touching it. I see the filthy edge of the once-white pyjama bottoms, and below that, the fair hairs which grow from her exposed calves. Her hips are narrow and wrong-looking, as if her legs have been attached at a strange angle. At the waistband, there is a gap where her stomach doesn't meet the material. She seems a different person, half the size of the girl I just saw tucked into bed: only the pyjamas are the same.

She watches me, crossing her arms. I'm excited to show her the cigarettes.

I hold out my hand: the two white sticks quiver.

She smiles and her face becomes hers again for a moment. Reaching forward, she hugs me, pressing her thin arms around me and squeezing. I close my fingers around the cigarettes, protecting them.

We sit on the edge of the bed.

She puts the cigarette in her mouth and flicks the lighter easily. Her silver ring gleams. Inhaling, she smiles.

I light my own cigarette, feeling the smoke fill me up.

She reaches forward, puts her free hand around my face, cups it, and rubs my cheek with her finger.

I look at the clock resting on the floor. It is a big yellow circle, with a smiley face. The hand that counts the seconds is broken, but I can still see the nub of it moving round and round. It's two o'clock. Not time for a cigarette, time for an afternoon nap.

I hear a sound and my heart leaps.

Kylan appears in the bedroom doorway. I breathe out. He seems tentative, as if he is unsure whether he wants to come looking for me.

I don't hide the cigarette, watching the shock flash across his face. I think how much he looks like his father.

'Mum, what are you doing?'

'I'm having a cigarette, darling.'

'You don't smoke.'

'There's a lot you don't know about me.'

The cigarette is burning away, but I can't bring myself to take a drag in front of him.

Kylan just stares.

'Are you all right, Mum?' he says eventually. His face crumples with worry, and I can't bear it. I reach forward, open the window, and drop the cigarette out.

'I'm fine, darling,' I say, putting my finger to my lips. 'It's my little secret. Don't tell your father.'

I reach my arms out for him and he allows himself to be pulled into a hug, flinching from the smell. Once his body is against mine, I don't want to let him go. I hold on, eventually feeling his arms over mine, pushing me gently backwards.

'What's the matter, Mum?' he says, squeezing my arms.

'I miss you,' I say.

'I miss you too,' he says, but he avoids making eye contact.

'Are you sure you're making the right decision?' I ask.

Kylan looks confused. 'What do you mean?'

'With Katya.'

He lets go of my arms. 'Of course I am,' he says.

'It's just that—'

'Look, Mum,' he says, 'you don't even know her. I love her, and you need to start making an effort with her because I'm going to marry her. I won't let you do this again.'

I feel my eyes widen. 'Do what again?'

Kylan sighs. 'It's like when I started seeing Vara. You had known her her whole life: she grew up down the road. But you still managed to scare her away.'

'Vara deserted you when you were being bullied,' I say.

'I wasn't being bullied.' He sounds angry. 'I got into a fight over a seat on the bus.'

I can't believe he is this self-deluded. 'You had a bloody nose, Kylan,' I say. 'The other boy hit you.'

'I hit him back,' he says. 'I've told you this so many times. It was a one-off.'

I remember all those days Kylan walked silently, head down, back to the house. Vara's face: those green eyes, her dark hair blowing in the wind by the side of the road where they got off the bus. I remember shouting at her that she should have been a better friend to Kylan. How could she just give up on him like that? They had been friends since they were children.

'She lost interest in being with you when things got hard,' I say.

Kylan looks at his feet. 'That wasn't because of the fight,' he says slowly.

'It was because she was a bad friend. You don't want people like that in your life, Kylan.'

'It was because you yelled at her. In front of a bus full of people. Of course she didn't want anything to do with me after that.'

I sink onto the bed. 'That's not what happened, Kylan,' I say, tears in my eyes again. 'I was protecting you.'

'I didn't need protecting,' he says. 'And I don't need protecting now. I love Katya, and I'm going to marry her. You need to start being nicer to her. Or—' He stops.

'Or what?' I say.

He pauses. 'Or we won't come here any more.'

I put my face in my hands. Eventually, he sits on the bed and puts his arm around me. 'I'm only asking that you give her a chance,' he says.

'I am,' I say, my voice a protest. He begins to shake his head. 'All right,' I say quickly, 'all right.'

'I love her, Mum,' he says. 'You need to accept that.'

I put my head on the shoulder of his shirt and rub my wet cheek against it. I take his hand in mine and squeeze it. He squeezes back. 'Let's go back down,' he says. 'We were worried about you.'

11

We enter the living room together, Kylan's hand on my lower back.

Hector passes me a glass of champagne and I sip it.

'Dinner should be ready soon,' I say, 'if you want to come with me.'

They follow me out of the room and across the hall, carrying their champagne glasses. The rectangular table is covered with a clean white tablecloth. The cutlery reflects the candlelight, and the plates shine like polished moons. I don't remember lighting the candles.

I have to admit, I've outdone myself.

Hector helps Matilda into her seat. Kylan sits next to his father in the seat he has had since he was a boy, and he pulls out the chair next to him for Katya. I smile at her, and she looks at Kylan and then smiles back.

Everyone oohs and aahs as they take their seats. I don't say anything.

Hector stands at the head of the table, holding his champagne flute aloft.

'I would like to propose a toast,' he says. 'To Katya and Kylan, and a long and happy marriage.'

He looks tall, looming above us. He is wishing them everything he wanted for us.

The others raise their glasses. My knuckles turn white around mine.

'We're so proud of you, Kylan,' he continues, 'and I'm so happy you've found such a wonderful partner.'

I carry through the bowls of potato soup from the kitchen. They steam: creamy brown and thick and whole-some, decorated with paint swirls of crème fraîche and chopped green chives.

'Have you set a date?' Matilda asks as I put down the last bowl of soup.

I see their hands linked together under the table, skirted by the delicate edge of the tablecloth.

'We were thinking next summer,' Katya says. 'We're hoping for nice weather.'

'Where are you planning on having it?' Matilda says.

'In the church where my parents got married,' she says. 'It's near my family house and we were thinking of having a reception outside in the garden there.'

'Katya has a beautiful house right on the edge of a fjord,' Kylan says. 'It's where I proposed.'

I swallow down a hot mouthful of soup.

'Where are you from, Katya?' I ask.

'Over on the west coast,' she says, smiling.

'And do you go back there a lot?' I ask, looking straight at Kylan.

'We fly over every month or two for a weekend,' he says.

'That's a long way,' I say.

'Not when you fly,' he says. 'We got the train once and that was stupid. By the time we got there we had to turn around and come back again.'

'It's further than it is to get here,' I say. No one says anything: I listen to the chink of the metal spoons against the china. 'Do they know,' I ask, 'about the engagement?'

'We went and told them last weekend,' Katya says, smiling widely. 'They were thrilled. They love Kylan.'

I put down my spoon, feeling the nausea return.

'My mother has already started planning,' Katya says. 'She's got all these ideas about a fancy reception, but I've told her all we really want is a small thing outside, with our closest friends.' I wish she would stop talking. 'But I've got quite a large family so I imagine it will end up bigger than we think.'

'Can I ask what's wrong with the church where your father and I got married?' I ask Kylan.

Katya's smile falters.

'It doesn't really make sense,' Kylan says. 'There's not that many on our side to invite, and Katya has such a big family, it's silly to make them travel all this way.'

'My mum has five brothers!' Katya exclaims, like this is a joke.

'All your family live on the west coast?' I ask.

Katya's smile wavers again. 'Well, not all, but—'

'Your grandmother got married in the same church as your father and I. It's really a lovely church. Your family might enjoy coming to this side of the country.'

There is a silence.

'Will your parents have far to come, Mrs Bjornstad?' Katya asks.

I stare at her. 'My name is Marta,' I say, my voice terse. 'And my parents are dead.'

Katya's smile completely disappears. I almost want to smile then myself.

I get up and start clearing the table. Carrying the bowls into the kitchen, I notice that Kylan and Katya's hands are no longer intertwined.

*

I put the dishes on the sideboard.

Shutting my eyes, I hear the sound of footsteps echoing across stone, and I am in the church where Hector and I got married, walking down the aisle. Matilda had shown me how: step left, step together, step right.

Hector's parents were our only guests. I could see Matilda standing in the front row, watching me, her face covered by the netting of her pale pink hat. Hector's father was already ill then, sunk in his seat. Every time we were left alone, all I could think about was the cancer eating away at his pancreas behind his suit, and I struggled to think of things to say. He would just smile at me, a tired, knowledgeable smile, as if every young woman was the same, and he had seen so many like me in his life that he couldn't bring himself to have that same old conversation again.

And there it is again, that strange echoing fear, slipping through the cracks that have formed in the memory. It's easy to look at a photograph, and to tell yourself things happened a certain way, that you were happy. Easy to talk about it until it seems that it really happened that way. But as I looked out through that gauzy veil, the petals of my bouquet quivering in my hands, as I made those steps towards Hector standing at the altar without my father's arm to support me, I remember being frightened, not excited.

We didn't have a reception: everyone agreed it would only upset me, not having my family there. We signed the marriage register straight after the ceremony. I looked down at Hector's signature, his small, neat handwriting still unfamiliar then. I wrote my new name as neatly as I could, remembering all the times I had practised it. *Mrs Marta Bjornstad.* I was her now.

When I turn around, Hector is standing in the doorway, his arms folded. I jump, putting my hand up to my chest.

'You scared me,' I say.

Hector doesn't move.

I start to pull bowls out of the cupboard for the halibut stew.

'Marta,' he says.

'What?'

'This needs to stop.'

I stare at him.

'Leave her alone,' he says. 'She only wants you to like her.'

I watch my unsteady hand as I ladle the stew from the pot to the first bowl.

'Kylan is going to marry her,' he says. 'He's happy. Can't you see how important that is?' His eyes are dark, clouded.

I take a deep breath. 'Don't you think they're too young?'

'You were younger than him when we got married.'

'That's different.'

We stare at each other.

'Can't you see how good it is, that he's found some-one? We both know it's not easy.'

The bowl begins to wobble in my hands. 'I just think he should wait a bit, until he's older,' I say.

'He might not have that many more chances,' Hector says. I focus on keeping the bowl still, on not spilling a drop. 'It's his decision,' he says. 'Did you ever think that maybe this was why he didn't tell you about the engagement? He didn't want you getting involved. You can never let him make his own decisions, stand on his own two feet.'

I slam the bowl down. Spots of creamy liquid dot the counter. 'I get it, Hector. You always know what's good for him, what he wants, and I don't. I understand.'

Hector sighs behind me. 'You just don't listen to him.'

'How can I listen to him if he never tells me any-thing?' I can hear the tears in my voice.

Hector comes and stands behind me. 'I know you don't want to lose him,' he says. 'But you're pushing him away. It's not fair. He only wants to be happy.'

I want to throw one of the bowls against the wall.

'Will you please take this through?' I say. I hold it out

to him. *Don't let your husband lift a finger: treat him as you would any other guest in your home.* 'I'll bring the rest.' After a moment, he takes the bowl, turns around and leaves the kitchen. I feel myself sink against the counter, my head in my hands.

I know she's there before I pull my hands away. She is lying on the kitchen floor, smoking a cigarette, her thin legs crossed over each other awkwardly. Her hip bones are still visible, but there's more of her stomach than there was the last time I saw her, and her hair is not as tangled and broken. She blows smoke rings at me.

There are seven piles of cards on the floor next to her in a line, some facing up, and some down.

She smiles. There is a black hole between her gums round the side: a tooth is missing. I run my tongue across my own teeth, but they're all there. She reaches forward to move a card to another pile, to turn one over.

When I open my eyes, I am sitting at the kitchen table, a lit cigarette between my fingers. My throat burns, and the room is filled with smoke, either hers or mine. I put my hand up to the tightness in my chest, my breaths rising hard and fast. What was I thinking? I have no idea where the cigarette has come from, and no recollection of lighting it. This is different, I think, to the other things I have been seeing. This is dangerous.

Standing up, I look around the kitchen, unsure what to do with the burning cigarette. I can hear the laughter in the dining room, and I wonder how long I have been in here. Sliding open the patio doors, I slip out and drop the cigarette into the drain.

I wonder if Hector is right. Perhaps I need to take my pills.

My hands shake as I lift the remaining bowls out of the cupboard. Stacking them upside down on top of the saucepan lid, I carry the whole thing through to the dining room to serve it there, leaving the patio doors open but shutting the kitchen door.

12

When I re-enter the room, they are still talking about the wedding. I put down the saucepan and begin serving the food, handing it down the table. Thinking of the salt, I smile. *The first rule of being a good hostess is never to apologize for something that may otherwise go unobserved.*

'We were thinking of having a buffet,' Katya is saying. 'We'd really just like a barbecue, but my mum will never allow it.'

I clear my throat. 'Do you mind if we stop talking about the wedding?' I say.

Katya stares, blinking. Everyone is looking at me. Taking a mouthful of food, I can taste little but the salt.

'What do you do for a living, Katya?' I ask, when I can't stand the silence any longer.

'I work in advertising,' she says.

'Is that in an office?' I ask.

Katya nods. 'It's a small agency but we've done some quite big campaigns.'

'And do you think you will keep working once you are married?'

'Yes,' she says. 'We don't see the wedding changing that much in our lives really. We already live together.'

'But you want to have children?'

'When we are a bit older,' she says. 'I don't think we're ready for that yet. We're too selfish, I suppose.' She looks at Kylan and they laugh.

'And too young,' Hector says.

'I was younger than Katya when I had Kylan,' I say. 'You didn't think it was too young then, Hector.'

'It was different then,' Hector says. 'You didn't have a career.'

'But you won't work when you have children,' Matilda says.

'I might,' Katya says, 'when they are a little older. I haven't decided yet.'

'I think you're all getting a bit carried away,' Kylan says, smiling. 'We certainly aren't planning on any children for a good few years yet.'

'Having children is an amazing experience, though,' I say, looking at Kylan. 'It's just a shame they have to grow up.'

Kylan smiles and then looks down at his plate.

'It's inevitable,' Katya says. 'That's why I think I'd like to keep working.'

I stare at her. It feels like an attack, and I want to say something, but I have promised Kylan I will make an effort.

The only sound is the scraping of the metal cutlery against the china. It makes my stomach churn. Closing my eyes, I see a white plate, rimmed with blue flowers, a steaming mound of beef stew and mashed potato, enough to feed four men. His big hands dwarf the cutlery, scraping the plate clean; his teeth grind.

When I open my eyes, the guests are observing me, their faces turned towards me in the candlelight.

I see myself then, a blank-faced marionette, like the porcelain dolls in the cabinet in the hallway.

I wonder if I was talking, if I said something I shouldn't have.

'What?' I say abruptly, the word stuttering around the table.

There is a pause.

'Nothing, Mum,' Kylan says. 'We were just saying how good the food is.'

I think of the long trail of white salt, disappearing below the surface of the stew. Why are they lying to me?

They watch as I sip my champagne.

Hector is staring at me, a warning look, and the fear tightens in my stomach. I need to behave myself.

Once everyone is finished, I get up and start clearing the bowls. Walking through to the kitchen, I keep checking to see if Hector has followed me, but he doesn't come.

I remember his hand on my back in the shady hallway of the hotel we stayed in on our honeymoon. It was dim compared with the sunshine reflecting off the outside paintwork, making the trees around the fjord paint the water with sparkling green.

The hotel was only a short drive from the chapel, and I was still wearing my wedding dress: I remember the difficulty of climbing the wooden stairs without tripping. There was champagne in an ice bucket in our bedroom and a fruit basket wrapped in cellophane on the dressing table. Hector locked the door to the room from the inside, then walked out onto the balcony. I began unwrapping the fruit, the plastic creaking under my fingers.

'Don't open that now,' Hector called through from the balcony, 'we'll go for dinner soon. Come out and look at the view.'

I followed him, resting my small hands on the white wooden rail next to his larger ones. The fjord stretched before us, and from the darkness of the water, I could tell it was deep. There was barely a ripple on the silky surface, and the valley was deserted.

I felt Hector watching me as I looked out. He moved

behind me, putting his hands on either side of mine and pressing his body into my back.

'My parents stayed in this room after their wedding,' he said. 'I always wanted to bring my wife here one day.'

I wished he hadn't mentioned his parents. I imagined his mother, before she was the stern woman I knew now, opening a neatly packed suitcase on the bed, folding her gloves one on top of the other on the dressing table. Pulling out a tissue from the luxuriously decorated tissue box and dabbing at her make-up, her face shiny after the long journey. It wasn't our room any more.

'It's a beautiful view,' I said, reaching up to kiss the side of his face.

'Well, we have it all to ourselves,' he said, and I could hear him smiling.

He took my hand and led me into the room, pushing me backwards onto the bed. Gently, he touched the material of the wedding dress that had once been his mother's. He sat there for a long time, just looking. I tried to reach up and kiss his cheek, but he pushed my head to the side and into the bed, keeping his eyes only on the dress. I heard the jangle of his belt buckle, and felt the dress being lifted up, my underwear pulled down around my knees. It took him some time to find his way. I tried to shift my body with his, to make it easier, but he put his hand over my hips and held me still as he jerked backwards and forwards. I watched the juddering lace of the canopy above. He moved faster and faster, muttering something that I couldn't make out, a word repeated over and over again.

He rolled onto his side afterwards, and I watched his pupils get smaller. Almost immediately, he sat up, and began to get dressed. The bed was damp between my legs, and I pulled my dress down, feeling a tear roll down the side of my face.

Hector went to stand at the window, a shadow against the bright outside light.

I tried not to make any sound.

'We'll go for a walk before dinner,' he said.

I pulled myself up. Hector turned and looked at me. He came closer, kneeling on the floor at my feet.

'You look amazing in that dress,' he said, 'Mrs Bjornstad.'

Through the kitchen door, I can hear them laughing in the dining room. I can still hear Hector's voice, close in my ear.

I take the ramekins of chocolate mousse out of the fridge and line them up neatly on a tray with a jug of cream. Each time I pick them up, one or other of the ramekins falls out of their neat formation, and I have to stop and straighten them again. *Presentation is every-thing: a meal must look appetizing to be appetizing.* I pick up the tray; it happens again. I slam the tray down onto the counter: the ramekins clash together and some of the cream escapes from the jug. My hands are trembling now: I hold them out in front of me, trying to steady them. I dig my fingers into my palms until my raw fingernails ache: until I feel like my fingers might break.

*

I pass the ramekins around the table, watching Kylan dig his spoon into his chocolate pot, making a dip which he fills with cream, just as he has always done.

'How is everything at school, Hector?' Matilda is asking.

'Oh, you know,' he says, 'same old.' Hector is look-ing down at his dessert.

'Did you know that Hector is a teacher, Katya?' Matilda asks. Katya nods. 'The pupils just love him. Don't they, Hector?' Matilda places her hand on Hector's arm, squeezing it. I fight the urge to bat it away.

'I don't know about that, Mother,' he says.

'Oh, Hector,' she says, 'don't be modest.' Matilda turns to Katya again. 'He's so dedicated to helping them achieve their goals.'

'Where do you teach, Hector?' Katya asks, chocolate on her front teeth. Her pink tongue emerges quickly and it is gone.

'At a school across the valley,' he says.

'You should see his notice board upstairs, Katya,' Matilda says. 'It's covered with notes from his students.' She turns to Hector. 'Show her after dinner, Hector. She'd like that.'

I see Hector, striding through the fading sunlight past the bleached brick of the school building, a book under his arm. I am watching through the car window, and he doesn't see me: I am parked out of sight. It is after hours: Kylan is at some after-school activity at the high school, and though I wasn't sure where I was going when I set off from the house, I am not surprised to find myself here.

It was a long time until I saw him walk out of the building again, and most of the other cars were gone. He wasn't alone: there was a student with him, a girl who must have been in the final year. I wondered if this was the girl he had told me about, the one who *had potential*, his latest after-school project. They stood on the steps, talking, her face leaning in close as if she was telling him a secret. Then she smiled a shy half-smile, and turned away. Hector took hold of her arm, and pulled her towards him, and for a split second, they embraced.

The girl turned away from him then, walking straight past my car without seeing me, her face flushed. Hector went the other way, getting into his car and pulling out of the car park.

I stand up. Everyone turns away from Hector to look at me. He must have been telling a story.

My head rings and I need to lie down, to think it over.

With unsteady hands, I collect the ramekins back onto the tray and walk back through to the kitchen.

'Is she all right?' I hear Matilda asking, but I keep walking.

'She's fine, Mother,' Hector says.

In the kitchen, I put the tray down and lean over the sink, taking deep breaths. I shut my eyes, trying to bring back the memory, to examine whether it was real or not. But I know that it is: I can feel the uncomfortable warmth from the car heaters, and see Hector's hands around the girl's waist.

I hear the door open behind me. I turn around, and Hector is there.

'Marta,' he says, 'I don't know what's going on with you, but I wish you would pull yourself together. You are ruining the evening.'

I want to confront him, to ask him about the girl I saw him with, about the others. But I hear the rumble of Kylan's voice from the dining room, Katya's laughter, and I don't want to cause a scene.

He stands in the doorway, staring at me, a little stooped, his hair more greying than I remember. He looks pitiable, and before I can stop myself I feel the laughter rising. No one is going to find him attractive any more, I think. That's when I realize I don't care; he can have all the students he likes.

'What are you laughing about?' he says, moving towards me.

My heart beats faster, but I can't stop.

'Marta, what the hell is so funny?'

I feel his growing anger almost as if it is my own: I know I am on unstable ground.

'Marta, stop it.'

He has hold of my arm now.

'What the hell is wrong with you tonight?'

There is a sound in the doorway and he turns his head. Katya is standing there, watching us. Hector lets go of my arm.

Her mouth is open and it takes a moment for her to say anything. 'I was just looking for the toilet.'

'It's down the hall on the left,' Hector says, and I can hear the effort it has taken to keep his voice level.

Katya nods, and turns away.

Hector turns back to me, his face red.

'Now see what you've done,' he says. 'Can't you behave yourself when we have guests?'

My smile edges in again: I feel as if I am not a part of this situation.

'I'll do the washing up,' I say, turning on the taps at the sink.

He stands there for some time.

'Go and see the others,' I say. 'They'll be wondering where we've got to.'

Eventually, I hear his footsteps retreating.

Through the crack in the kitchen door, I see the shadowy figures go into the living room, and hear a CD begin to play on the stereo. I work my way through the washing up slowly. Below the surface of the water, below the soap suds, I feel something stringy and wet floating, like seaweed, brushing past my hands. I feel around under the surface, and the substance becomes thicker, filling the sink. Pulling my hands out, I realize the sink is full of hair, matted together in clumps, enough hair to fill the entire bowl. It wraps itself around my hands: I try to free my fingers but they are caught. Dimly, I remember the feeling of wet hair under my fingers: I feel a shooting pain in my neck.

'Marta?'

I look up. She is leaning against the frame of the kitchen doorway, watching me, wearing a big red coat with the hood pulled up. Her blonde hair escapes from the sides of the material and her cheeks are flushed with cold. She carries a sports bag and I can see her peach tights protruding from the bottom of the coat. She is smiling her wide white smile.

'How do you know that name?' I say.

She stares. She is wearing black eyeliner. She looks so young.

'I thought you wanted me to call you Marta,' she says. I blink, and Katya is standing there, in her flowery dress. She looks confused.

I look down at the sink. My hands are still below the surface of the water, but there is nothing there.

'Did you want something?' I say.

'I just came to see if you needed any help,' she says.

'It's fine. Go back in there and enjoy yourself.'

'Are you sure?'

'Yes,' I say.

She is still standing there. 'Marta?' she asks. 'I'm so sorry I asked about your parents. I didn't know.'

No, I think, *you don't know.*

'It's fine,' I say. 'Honestly. It was a long time ago.'

'It must have been hard, to hear me talk about the

wedding preparations if your parents weren't there for yours,' she says. 'I'm sorry.'

She's trying to bond with me, and it makes me sick. I want to push her out of the room and shut the door.

'Really, Katya,' I say. 'Don't worry about it.'

She turns to leave and then stops. 'And thanks again for dinner. It was delicious.'

No it wasn't, I want to shout. I step towards her and grasp hold of her hand. And there it is again: her ring. She stares back at me, wide-eyed.

'Katya,' I say. 'Are you sure you want to do this?'

'Do what?' she says.

'Get married.'

She looks down at my hand, over hers. 'I'm really excited about it,' she says. 'I love Kylan.'

I let go of her. 'It's your decision too,' I say. 'Just remember that.'

'I love Kylan,' she says. I want to shake her.

I look into the water in the sink.

'Are you all right, Mrs Bjornstad?'

I wipe my eyes. 'I'm fine,' I say. 'Please don't tell Kylan I said anything.'

When she is gone, my hands are shaking, the rage vibrating through my body. I shut my eyes, but all I see is her young, perfect face, smiling sweetly back at me.

I imagine them having their own children, a little boy like Kylan, a little girl with blonde hair: I see a perfect family picture. And I will always be on the outside.

Behind my eyes, the family picture refuses to fade. A man and a woman stand arm in arm under a wide dark tree, the sunlight in their faces. The man's hair is sandy, split down the middle like Kylan's, but the woman is different to Katya, her hair darker and longer, her feet bare. Between them stands a girl in her early teens, smiling, wincing at the camera, her features erased by the light. The picture begins to dim, and I cling to it, longing to understand who the people are. There's a roaring sadness in my chest that feels as if it is pressing to escape, and I lean against the sink, waiting for it to pass.

My hand reaches out for the phone on the kitchen wall. The numbers are there, on the edge of my mind, and I type them in fast, before they fade again. I hold the phone up to my ear. It rings and rings but there is no answer.

I put down the phone and pick it up again, but when I try to remember the number, it is gone. For a long time, I screw my eyes tight shut, willing the picture back, but it doesn't come.

Eventually, I take another bowl and continue with the washing up.

Once the house is back to normal, I go to the living room. The CD has been turned off and the television is on.

I tell them I am going to bed, and head upstairs.

13

I check the rooms, laying clean towels on each of the beds. Normally, I would put a hot-water bottle under Kylan's sheets for him to find, but I see Katya's suitcase on the floor of the guest bedroom and I know I can't do that any more.

In the bathroom, I fill the basin with water, shut my eyes, and wash my face. I rub my face on a towel, and when I look up, she is there in the mirror next to me. Her hair is still white blonde: a little greasy, and tied in a shiny ponytail. She wears the pyjamas with the pink hearts, but they are clean now. Side by side, her leg is wider, denser, than mine. She hasn't lost the weight yet. I put my hand out, squeezing the hard muscle. She tenses her leg, stretching it out and pointing her toes. Then she begins the exercises: swinging her leg out to the side, the front, and then the back, pushing it up as far as it will go. As she lifts her arms, they are inches from my face, her fingernails unbitten.

I begin to copy her and our movements align, our legs next to each other. She can get hers higher than mine, much higher; her movements are more fluid. We rise onto our tiptoes, and I feel my muscles elongate. I touch the ceiling and hold, hold, hold.

When I lower myself back down, she is gone. My heart pounds in my chest; my arms and legs tingle.

Entering the bedroom, I look around to check if she is still there. Though I can't see her, I feel her watching me as I undress and pull my woollen nightgown over my head. I slip under the covers and shut my eyes, trying to ignore the sounds from downstairs, to drift off to sleep.

*

I wake up to screaming in the darkness. It is loud, piercing. Soon, the sounds turn into words. *Help me, somebody, please.* Sometimes it stops, and beyond it, through the silence, I can hear the whirring of a fan. Then it starts again.

'Marta?'

I blink in the darkness, not sure whether my eyes are open or shut. There is the familiar sense of dread.

The light flicks on. The clock on the bedside table reads 03:07. Hector is beside me in the bed, his eyes bleary with sleep, flat and unreadable.

'You were screaming,' he says, as though he knows he doesn't need to.

I feel the softness of the ironed sheets, the warmth of the bedside lamp.

'I'm sorry,' I say. It's the old conversation, and I remember my part.

'Bad dream?' he asks.

I think, as if I can't remember, then nod. I don't think I was asleep at all.

'Do you want to talk about it?' he says. He has learnt, by now, that the answer is always no.

'I'm fine,' I say.

He looks at me one last time, then rolls onto his back. 'Do you think you'll be able to get back to sleep?' he asks.

'Yes,' I say, and Hector flicks out the light.

I lie in the yawning darkness. My stomach is heavy, as if it is filled with jagged black stones. I raise my hand up to my face, but I see nothing and I squeeze my eyelids together to check they are closed. I count to a hundred. I do it again. Nothing changes.

Then I hear her voice, whispering: her breath is warm in my ear.

They'll never find me. I don't even know where I am.

Then she is screaming again.

I can't stand it. With my head resting on the pillow, I put my fingers in my ears.

When I pull my hands away, she has stopped. There is only silence now, and that is worse, because it means she has gone again.

14

The light begins to glow at the edge of the curtains, tattooing the wall with squares of blue. My face feels tight and achy in the dim bedroom.

Walking down the stairs, I open the front door. Outside, the world is white. Our stretch of drive, usually so flat and grey, is covered: the cars a line of freshly made beds. Bright blue morning light reverberates, leaving no room for darkness; it spreads across the fields, masking where the hills begin, where they meet the sky. The flat bowl of the valley is marked out by spindly telephone poles, fences, and the low-hovering ghosts of leafless bushes and trees: white shadows of the former world.

Winter has come suddenly and my world is no longer the same place. The air out here feels brand new: I need to be where everything is hidden, away from the staleness of the house.

I pull my snow boots out of the hall cupboard, lacing them around my bare legs, then slip into Hector's huge cushioned green coat. It smells of dried dampness: of spruce needles and a thousand winter walks.

The snow sticks to my boots, leaving a heavy black trail. It's not too thick on the ground yet, just enough to cover everything. I use my sleeve to remove the worst of it from the windscreen and climb in, rolling down the windows, turning on the engine, surprised when it fills the air with sound. The snow crunches under the tyres: I should put the chains on. If I get myself stuck, Hector will be angry.

I pull out into the lane, indistinguishable from the fields around it. White-trimmed fences mark out where I should manoeuvre the car, though I almost lose my bearings several times. Once I am out on the bigger roads, tyres of earlier cars have marked out straight grey paths through the whiteness. I follow them, starting to increase my speed, feeling the chilled rush of the wind. I drive faster.

The glow of the shop emerges out of the lowering fog. My headlights make it swirl, the light losing itself in the opaque white air. When I turn off the engine, the silence is total. Sweat prickles under the neck of my jacket. Even if I were to scream at the top of my lungs, I know that the sound wouldn't be heard.

Taking a deep breath, I open the car door. The

cold wind hits me. I move towards the square of yellow light.

The door is heavy and as I lean against it, a bell rings through the silence, making me jump. I clomp across to the refrigerator and pull out a large carton of milk. I see her reflected in the glass doors: the messy hair, the purple marks under her eyes like bruises, white pyjamas, bare feet. I turn away and look back quickly but it is only me in the reflection: a middle-aged woman, swamped by a huge coat over her nightdress.

The man at the counter is watching me. His dark hair is flattened by his hat and his ears are red; he is still wearing his jacket and gloves. He has a dark little brush of a moustache and his smile tremors beneath it like something hiding under the bed.

I put the milk onto the counter, feeling the sweat on my hands as his moustache lifts into a smile.

Once I have handed him the money, he gives me my change. Soon, I am out in the snow, the wind whipping my hair out of my face. I get back into the car quickly.

A red vehicle comes out of the white fog: bumper glinting silver, huge headlights sending out tunnels of yellow. Scraping metal, a heavy thumping: the sounds of spraying grit escaping onto the road. The noises stay, changing, getting louder as the gritter retreats. Even when it is gone, I still hear the horrible familiar churning of stone against stone, of darkness moving, over and over. Shoving my fingers in my ears, the sounds fill my head.

Through the fog, the light of the shop flickers for a moment. I shut my eyes, but the light remains, intensifying into a long bar, flashing into life. A sharp pain twinges in my temples, behind my eyes, travelling round the back of my head. It is an electric strip light, running across a grey ceiling. As if I am getting used to the new light, the room begins to form: the bed, the toilet, the sink. I see her, tucked into the bed sheets, blinking, her black eyeliner smudged.

I follow her gaze back to the ceiling, where the sounds were coming from. The edges of a metal door begin to drop, jerking awkwardly. A square of dim light appears slowly. Then the ladder. Cargo pants streaked with white dust. A faded green shirt with a rip at the elbow and paint splattered across the front. The brown hair at the back of his head.

He stops on the ladder and pulls the door shut, clicking the padlock into place. He puts a key on a yellow key ring into his breast pocket.

At the bottom of the steps, he turns around. She looks up at him.

'In this room,' he says, 'you must keep your eyes down.'

She shifts her eyes to the ground, looking at his boots. The big metal eyelets, the brown laces, tied in neat double knots. He stands above her, his head almost grazing the ceiling.

The boots walk over to the chair. He sits down.

Standing again, he reaches out and places his hand on a crack on the wall above his head, as if he is rubbing the flank of an animal.

'I hope you like the room,' he says.

She keeps her eyes on the grey carpet.

'What's your name?' he asks.

She can't answer.

He takes something out of the pocket of his cargo pants.

'I can't give you this unless you tell me your name,' he says. 'I want us to get along.'

She lets her eyes flick upwards: it is a chocolate bar. Her stomach growls.

'I know you're hungry,' he says. 'It will be much easier if we can be friends.'

Eventually, the boots move towards the ladder. He stops.

'It's your choice,' he says. 'Just remember that.'

Then he slips the chocolate bar back into his pocket and climbs the ladder, pulling it up after him. As the door is shutting, she gets up from the bed, tries to reach up after it. It swings shut, jarring into place. She jumps and her fingers graze the top of it, but it is closed now. She sits back onto the edge of the bed. After a long time, she begins to mutter something under her breath, closing her eyes tight. I strain to make out the words.

Elise, Elise, Elise.

And then there is only the whirr of the car heaters, the whiteness outside, and the lights of the shop. I can't see the car or the road or the trees or the mountains.

I listen for her, and I think I make out her voice, floating in the dense air.

Please let me go.

Just let me go.

Please.

I sit there for a long time, listening. She can't hear me, and after a while I stop trying to make her.

*

The house glows through the white that has fallen on the valley. I see the lights before anything else, vague yellowness emerging through the car windscreen.

As I climb the steps to the front door, I decide that

Kylan and Katya can't go back today. I know it's not too bad, but it's bad enough. We'll all have to stay put: shut out the cold. The house will be filled with noise and life again.

As I open the door, I smell bacon. In the kitchen, Matilda is at the stove, wearing my red apron. Hector is sitting at the table, reading the paper. There is a clutter of pans, utensils, and bowls on the surface and the hob is spotted with grease. I sigh inwardly, knowing I will have to clear it up later. I want to tell them to get out.

'Where's Kylan?' I ask.

'In the living room,' Matilda says. She opens the cupboard above the sink. 'I don't know why you had to move things around. I can't find anything.'

Hector looks up.

'Have you been out dressed like that?'

I look down at my wet nightgown, the huge coat.

'I went to get some milk,' I say.

He leans over and opens the fridge door. 'We have plenty of milk,' he says. 'We'll end up throwing half of it away, as usual.'

'We have guests,' I say.

Hector stares at me. 'They're leaving today,' he says.

'I think they should stay here,' I say, looking at my bitten fingernails.

'What do you mean?'

'It's too dangerous.'

'Marta, it's only the first snow,' he says. 'A light dusting.'

'There's a fog,' I say.

'It's forecast to get worse tonight. They wanted to go when they woke up, but they didn't want to miss you.'

'Don't you want them to stay?' I ask.

He sighs. 'Of course I do, Marta, but they've got lives to get back to.'

'Aren't you worried about the snow, Matilda?' I say.

Matilda looks up from the stove. 'Why would I be? It's not even bad yet.'

I sit down at the kitchen table, my hands in my lap. I imagine reaching forward and smashing Hector's head onto the table, over and over.

There are little etchings of frost on the window which I trace with my fingers. Hector has gone back to his paper. Matilda concentrates on frying the bacon, curling patches of wet pink leather. I remember that my fingertip might leave a mark on the window and stop.

'I still think it would be safer if Kylan stays one more night,' I say.

Hector doesn't look up. 'We'll see what he says.'

Just then, I hear Kylan in the hall. I go to the kitchen door. He is pulling on his coat.

'Where are you going?' I say.

'I'm just going to put the snow chains on,' he says. 'We should probably get going after breakfast.'

'It's dreadful out there,' I say. 'Perhaps you should stay here tonight.'

'It's not too bad,' he says. 'And we have work tomorrow.'

I put my hand on Kylan's arm. 'Don't you think you should wait until the snow passes?'

'They say it's only going to get worse.'

'Then you should probably stay here,' I say.

'We can't, Mum,' he says. 'You know that.'

Matilda calls through from the kitchen. 'Breakfast's ready.'

Hector comes through with two plates and hands one to Kylan. 'Shall we eat in the living room? Marta, yours is in the kitchen.'

Kylan nods and they head in. Matilda carries two plates through from the kitchen.

I stand in the hall for a long time, listening to the chatter continue in the other room, before I follow them.

The living room is warm: Hector has lit the fire, and there is the sound of wood cracking in the fireplace. *Always light the fire in the winter: make the home as cosy as possible for your family to enjoy.* It seems like without me, everything has continued as normal.

Katya is sitting on the sofa with Kylan. He looks up and sees me standing there.

'Not hungry?' he asks.

I don't answer.

There is nowhere for me to sit anyway.

After they have finished eating, I can feel the restlessness in the room rising. Everyone is getting ready to leave. Kylan fetches the overnight bags and Hector leads Matilda out to her car. The front door is ajar, and a chill spreads through the room.

I cross my arms, moving to the small hall window. There are swirls of flakes dropping from the sky.

'It's snowing again,' I say, but no one is listening.

Kylan and Katya have their coats on. I stand rigidly in the middle of the hall.

'The roads are sure to be icy,' I say.

'The main ones will be gritted,' Kylan says. I think of the huge red gritter whirring past me on the side of the road and feel sick. He comes forward and embraces me stiffly. 'Thanks, Mum,' he says. 'We'll see you soon.'

'Thanks for having me, Mrs Bjornstad,' Katya says. She doesn't try to hug me, and I am glad.

'Please call me Marta,' I say. I look at Kylan. 'When are you coming back?' I say.

He runs his hand through his hair. 'A couple of

months,' he says. 'I'll let you know if we'll be back for Christmas.'

Hector comes back in from outside, blood high in his cheeks.

'Mother's safely in her car,' he says. 'The engine's running, and the windscreen is clear. Everyone ready to go?'

'Yeah,' Kylan says. He doesn't look at me.

I go through to the living room and look out of the window. Hector's mother is sitting with her hands on the wheel, and I can hear the dull moaning of the radio voices. I watch Kylan and Katya climb into Kylan's car, parked in front of Matilda's. Katya is laughing at something Kylan is saying.

Hector stands in the driveway, waving his big gloved hands as they drive out.

He is going now, I think, he is really going. I didn't do enough. He won't ever be coming back, not properly. I think of Hector and me in the house, indefinitely, trying to find things to fill the time, and I feel like a hand is closing around my throat.

The car headlights uncover hundreds of tiny white flakes, flying like insects in the light.

15

Standing by the window, watching the empty drive, I hear the front door slam. Hector comes into the room behind me and I quickly wipe away a tear.

He is still wearing his raincoat, the hood pulled up. Stopping by his armchair, he slips his gloves off his hands, one by one.

'I don't know what you're so upset about,' he says, his eyes dark. 'You made that dinner as difficult as you possibly could. I don't know how you expected them to stay longer.'

I stare at him.

'It's not just yourself you're ruining things for, you know,' he says. 'This is my family too.'

He takes a step towards me. 'I'm sorry,' I say, trying to keep the tears out of my voice. 'I wanted everything to be perfect.'

'I don't believe you,' he says. 'You need to let him live his own life. We've had our time, can't you see that? It's Kylan's turn to be happy.'

Are we happy? I think.

'You can never just make things easy,' he says.

Why can't you make things easy?

I'm doing this for both of us.

Hector's mouth doesn't move but the words echo around the living room, scattered with the remains of breakfast. Plates, crumbs, crushed cushions out of their places.

I stand there, in the light from the window, another tear coming. I have failed him again. I can never make him happy. No matter what I do, it will never be enough. And now Kylan is gone, and it's only Hector and me.

He turns and walks out of the room.

Once he is gone, I stand staring at the space where he was, feeling something black and ugly rise up in my chest. I see him again, outside the school, embracing the student. This is not all my fault, I think. I can't let him blame me for everything that is wrong.

A few minutes later, Hector comes back into the living room, holding two black bin liners.

'I'm going to take the recycling to Kistefoss,' he says.

I stay still, waiting for him to leave.

When he reaches the doorway, I can't bear it any more.

'I know, Hector,' I blurt.

He stops.

'You know what?'

'I know about the student.'

He tries to hide it, but I see him balk. 'How do you—' he starts. 'Who told you?'

I shrug, not wanting to give myself away.

'I was going to tell you,' he says. 'That's why I came home early on Friday. But I couldn't do it.'

'On Friday?'

He nods. 'How long have you known?'

'Not long.'

'I was due for retirement anyway,' he says.

I stare at him. 'What are you talking about?'

'The student,' he says. 'I've lost my job.' Something flashes across his face, something I try to get a grip on.

'You've lost your job? When?'

'A few months ago,' he says. 'I thought you said you knew.'

'I know about the student.'

'The one in final year that I was helping? It was misconstrued by the school.'

I reach for the edge of the bay-window seat and sit down.

'Marta?' Hector says.

He doesn't seem familiar to me any more.

'Who told you?' he asks.

I can't answer.

Hector comes and stands in front of me. 'It's not true.'

His eyes are clear and blue, unblinking.

'It hasn't been proven,' he says. 'They're investigating, but they won't find anything.'

'Who made the complaint?' I ask.

'That young teacher, Mr Dahler,' he says. 'He wanted my job.'

'And did the girl confirm it?' I ask.

'Of course not,' Hector says. 'It isn't true.'

'Is she all right?'

Hector looks confused. 'She's fine,' he says. 'Nothing happened. She's doing her final exams, but she'll do well: she's a bright girl.' There's a silence. 'You know I have a close relationship with some of my students,' he says. 'They depend on me. It was just misinterpreted.'

I want to believe him, but I remember what I saw, so many years ago. I begin to feel afraid.

'You've been off work for how long?' I say.

'About two months. I'm on suspension while they investigate.'

'Where have you been going every day?' I ask.

Hector sighs. 'The park, the market, the pub, anywhere I can think of. I wanted to tell you, but I couldn't. I don't know why.'

The thought of Hector lying to me, watching me at the market, in the house, makes my skin feel itchy.

'I'm not sure I can believe you, Hector,' I say.

His eyes darken. 'What do you mean?' he asks.

'You've been lying to me,' I say. 'This has been going on for two months, and you haven't told me about it. How am I supposed to trust you?' My heart is beating fast.

'You should know I would never lie to you,' he says. 'I didn't tell you because I didn't want you to think less of me. I'm supposed to be supporting this family and now I can't.'

I stare at him. 'I'm your wife,' I say. 'You should be able to tell me things like this.'

'Can't you see, that's the reason I couldn't tell you?' he says. 'Because you are my wife. I didn't want you to think that I had failed you.'

'It's the same as lying, Hector. If you didn't do anything, why wouldn't you just tell me?'

Hector stands silhouetted, his fists clenched.

'I need you to remember everything I have done for you. And Kylan.' He takes my hand. 'Please,' he says. 'I need you to trust me.'

I see my former self, lying in Hector's bed, while he sits with a tray on his knees and spoons food into my mouth, as if I am a baby.

I think again of the school steps. Of Hector pulling the girl towards him.

His hands are trembling. There's a pain in my chest.

'I saw you, Hector,' I say. 'I saw you outside the school.'

'What are you talking about?'

'I saw you with a student. Years ago. You hugged her outside the school.'

He stares at me, his eyes wide. Then his face changes, and he laughs, short and sharp. 'I hugged her?' he says. 'What does that even mean?'

'I think you were having an affair with her,' I say. 'And I think you've done it again. I think you've been doing it for years.'

'Marta,' he says, 'listen to yourself. You think that because you saw me *hugging* a student that I was sleeping with her. That I've slept with all my students. Can't you see how ridiculous that is? I'm old enough to be her father.'

I tell myself not to fall for it, that he is trying to trick me again.

'I don't think I can stay here,' I say.

'What do you mean?' he asks.

'I think I need to leave.'

Hector's face flushes. 'It's not true,' he spits. 'I'm really hurt that you can't believe me, Marta. After everything.

I took you in when no one else would. I made you better, and now you're going to leave me when I need you the most.'

We stare at each other, and I feel myself faltering. He steps towards me, grabbing hold of my arms.

'Think about it,' he says, his blue eyes steady. 'Why would I risk everything I have, you and Kylan, my job, my reputation, for a dalliance with a student. If you think about it rationally, you'll see it makes no sense.'

'But I saw you, Hector,' I say.

'You didn't see anything,' he says. 'You saw me hug a student. I wish I could tell you which student it was, or why I hugged her, but I can't. It was so long ago. Who knows whether you even saw it? We both know you have a vivid imagination.'

I remember the cigarettes I have found in my bag, in my hand, seemingly from nowhere; the girl who I have seen so many times now. I think of the line between Kylan's eyes.

Really, what else do I have left?

Finally, I nod my head.

Hector smiles. He stands in front of me, holding his arms out. I rest my head against his shoulder and breathe in his smell, feeling his arms close around my back. We stand there for a long time.

Eventually, Hector breaks away, picking up the bags of recycling. 'I'll take these now,' he says.

'Do you have to go?' I ask. I don't want to be alone. I am afraid that without Hector here to explain, I will start doubting him again.

'I won't be long,' he says. 'Then we can go for a walk in the snow. It looks like it's clearing up after all.'

I hold on to him, trying to push down my sense of unease.

Then he leaves, and it is just me and the house again.

*

Once everything is silent, there is little to do but pile up the plates. In the kitchen, I wash them with shaking hands. I collect the cloth and cleaning spray from under the sink.

The kitchen table reflects chunks of sky, and I am surprised to find no marks on the glass. I trace the surface until I find one. Smears rise up where the cloth has been, and I set to work rubbing it all clean. I don't notice the tears until a couple run off my face, mingling with the milky splatterings of polish. It is only when I feel them on my cheeks, wetting the skin, that I stop and reach my hand up. My damp fingertips taste salty.

I try to tell myself that I am being irrational, that Hector is right. It doesn't make any sense.

But I see her, in the half-light, raising her unmarked oval face to him. Her blonde hair glistens over her shoulders. Her hand, with the ring on the index finger, reaches up into his hair. Her fingernails are unbitten.

✳

Soon afterwards, Hector arrives back, true to his word. I have been sitting at the kitchen table, staring out at the patches of receding snow on the brown ground, trying to think of nothing at all. For some time, I have watched a magpie, working at the frozen earth.

We dress in our warmest clothes, putting on as many layers as we can. When we get to the hallway, Hector holds out my coat for me, slipping my arms in and then buttoning up the front. He laces my snow boots, then his own.

He takes my arm and we go out into the cold together, trudging towards the lane. Hector's stick leaves strange marks next to our footprints. We walk our old path, looking for tracks in the snow: I find some left by a bird in a field and he spots some footprints up near the farm. Hector uncovers a bench and we sit down.

The wind has made his cheeks red. He looks straight ahead, towards the distant fjord.

'Do you think they'll give you your job back?' I ask.

He looks at me. 'I don't want to go back there again,' he says, 'not after this.'

'Why not?'

'It wouldn't be the same,' he says. 'No one would trust me.'

He turns to face me then, his blue eyes watching me calmly, full of something raw, painful. It brings me back to the water underneath the surface of the sea on our holiday to the island. I remember the pressure in my nose and mouth, the tunnels of light fading towards the surface, the loosening of everything.

I see then how hard this must be for Hector. By suggesting he is at fault, by bringing his morality into question, they have broken the power he had over his students. Perhaps that's why he didn't tell me, because he was afraid of losing his power over me too.

'Are you going to get another job?' I ask.

'I don't think I'll be able to,' he says.

'Why not?'

He sighs. 'I suppose I'm too old now.'

'You're a good teacher, Hector,' I say.

'I've worked at that school for so long,' he says. 'Since before we met. It just feels like the end of my life.' He takes my hand, squeezes it. 'But at least I have you,' he says. 'It will be the start of a new chapter for us, with Kylan gone, and me retiring.'

As I watch him, I feel something around my neck, as if there are hands there, pushing against my voice box. I clear my throat and the feeling passes.

He gets up then, and begins walking back towards the house. I watch him, his back slumped, and then reach my arm out to help him.

*

When we get back, it's almost dark, and I am shivering from the cold, my teeth chattering. I tell Hector I am going to have a bath.

I turn on the taps and remove my clothes, feeling the hairs rise on my body. Once the bath is full, I lower myself in, leaning back and shutting my eyes.

I am still shivering, my body heavy and weak. My head feels dense, my eyelids weighted, as if a thick black fog has descended and I can't find my way out. Opening my eyes is difficult but I do so slowly, looking down at the narrow limbs, emerging from the murky water, bowing slightly at the top. The knees are big and bony, the breastbone and ribs visible through the white skin. I watch my chest rise and fall, rise and fall.

It is not my body.

I lift myself up, moving forwards with such force that water slops over the rim.

When the water has settled a little, I look down. My old body has returned: the fleshy legs and dimpling skin; the wrinkled stomach; my drooping breasts like rats' noses, pointing down into the water, which is still shifting against the sides of the bath. I try to slow my breathing, but I can't calm myself. Even though the moment has passed I can still see the fine hairs on her arms and legs, her chest moving with my breaths. This was different: for a few seconds, she wasn't just here, I was her: I knew how it felt to be her.

Hector comes running into the room.

'Is everything all right?' he says.

'It's nothing,' I say.

He looks confused. 'I heard you shouting. What happened?'

'I saw something,' I say.

'What?' he asks.

I shake my head. 'It wasn't anything,' I say. 'A trick of the light.' But I know I am not telling the truth. She was really here.

'Are you sure you've been taking your pills?' Hector says. 'You know what happens if you don't, how unstable you can get.'

'You saw me take them, Hector,' I say.

'Well, maybe they're not working any more. You're seeing things that aren't there.'

'Maybe they are there,' I say.

'Marta, listen to yourself. Do you think we should go and see someone?'

I don't know why he says we, he means me.

'I don't need to see anyone,' I say, my voice echoing around the bathroom.

'There's no need to shout,' he says.

'I wasn't, I just—'

'Look, Marta, I just want you back to normal,' he says. 'You haven't been yourself.'

I wonder what he means by that. Does he just like me quiet, drugged, agreeing with everything he says?

'What if I wasn't myself before?' I ask.

Hector frowns. 'Why are you asking all of these questions? Are you not happy here?'

I think of the house, of Kylan, of Hector. I nod.

'Perhaps I would be better if Kylan was at home,' I say.

'Marta, you know he can't come back here. He's getting married.'

'But if he was a little closer—'

'You have to let him go,' Hector says. 'Focus on our

lives now. I'll be home more now, and we can go on trips, like we did when we first met.'

I think of a hotel room, with a big bed and a view. A bathroom I don't have to clean. But there is still that tight feeling, the hands closing around my throat. Wherever we are, it will still be the same.

At last, I nod. He looks sad.

'This is a new beginning for us. You should be more excited.'

He bends down, taking my wet hand in his, staring at me. I can't look him in the eye.

'I can help you wash, if you like,' he says. 'Like I did in the old days.'

'It's OK,' I say. 'I'm getting out soon.'

He stays there, his hand still in mine.

'I love you, Marta,' he says.

I watch the water. I know what I need to say, but the words tangle together in my throat, refusing to come forward. 'I'll be down soon,' I say.

Hector drops my hand, and I watch his slippers move across the floor to the bathroom door. Once again, I have failed to give him what he needs.

16

Downstairs, Hector is standing by the microwave, reheating the remains of the halibut stew. I watch him remove the Tupperware container, flip off the lid with his nails and scoop the contents into two bowls.

He smiles when he sees me standing in the doorway.

We sit and eat in silence. The fish tastes better today, less salty.

My spoon feels strange in my hand: not right, too big, as if it has suddenly grown. I see another spoon for a moment, a child's spoon with a plastic handle. I look down, and the image disappears.

I take another mouthful of food. Soon, I am scraping the bottom of the bowl.

When we are both finished, I put our bowls by the sink and turn on the tap. Hector comes and stands behind me, puts his arms around my waist, takes my hand off the tap.

'Do it tomorrow,' he says.

I pause, and then I turn the tap off and pull the plug out. The water drains away.

He takes my hand and we walk through to the living room.

Hector turns on the television and we watch the news. I rest my head on his shoulder and imagine I can hear his heart beating.

If you do what I say, there's no reason for anyone to get hurt.

I sit up. 'What did you say?'

'What?'

'What did you just say?' My voice is sharp.

Hector looks at me strangely. 'I didn't say anything.'

I stare at him. I definitely heard the voice again, and it sounded familiar.

I stand up. 'I'm going up to bed,' I say.

'But it's only eight thirty.'

'I'm tired.'

'I thought we were having a nice time,' he says.

I walk towards the door.

In the kitchen, I wash the plates. Then I go to wipe down the kitchen table. As I rub the surface, it changes. It is white now, scratched. I look around the room at the grey concrete walls, the neatly made bed, the grey carpet. Wiping the table with a sponge, she looks up, but she doesn't notice me, glancing at the yellow clock. Seven twenty-five. Scrubbing desperately, she increases her speed.

Discarding the sponge, she puts down two place-mats. Then the cutlery, one pair for an adult, and one for a child. Two plates with a flowered rim. She fills two plastic beakers with water from the dirty sink.

There is the sound then: a terrible, heavy scraping. Dropping the sponge into the sink, she stands at the edge of the table and straightens one of the forks. Then she looks up at the trapdoor in the ceiling, and it begins to lower, spraying dirt into the room. Some lands in her hair but she doesn't brush it out.

She keeps her eyes on the floor as he descends the steps: first his brown boots, then his work trousers, then his green shirt, his brown hair. He's carrying a Tupper-ware container in his hands. I can't see his face; he takes the nearest chair, so that his back is facing me. He uses his long fingernails to flip the lid and spoons the brown stew onto the plates.

'Did you have a good day?' she says.

'Sit down,' he says.

She does.

He passes her the plate with less food in it.

She waits for him to start, tapping her spoon, then

eats with small, bird-like movements, chewing slowly. The restraint she uses reminds me of someone acting, not really eating.

When she's finished, she watches him eat.

'Can I have that?' she says, pointing at the centimetre of food left in the Tupperware box on the table.

He moves it away. 'No,' he says. 'You know how you get when you've had too much to eat.'

He scrapes his fork against the china, shovelling down the last mouthful.

'It smells of smoke in here,' he says. 'How many cigarettes do you have left?'

'I finished my last one today,' she says.

'Good,' he says. 'I'm not bringing you any more. It's disgusting in here. I don't know how you can live like this.' She looks at the table. 'Come on, then,' he says. 'I haven't got all day.'

She takes the dishes to the sink and washes them.

'Hurry up,' he says.

She dries them on a towel and hands them to him.

He gets up. He hands her a spoon and taps the top of the Tupperware box. 'I'll leave this for you,' he says. 'Just this once.'

She smiles. 'Thank you,' she says.

'But don't eat it all at once. I'll try and come again tomorrow but I might not be able to.'

'Do you want to play cards?' she says.

'I have to get going.'

'Chess?'

'No. It's enough that I come down here and eat with you.' He starts climbing the ladder. 'Clean this place up,' he says.

Once he's gone, she goes to the bed, puts her hand underneath the mattress and pulls out a packet of cigarettes, half full. She slides one out and lights it, breathing in deeply, her exhaled smoke blocking my view of her. I reach forward to waft it away, but she is gone, and I am back in the kitchen. I feel myself fall backwards onto one of the chairs. I can still hear his voice, vaguely familiar. Willing it back into the room, I try to work out where I have heard it before. The girl too is familiar. The things I have been seeing are too vivid not to be real: I feel what she must have felt, things I couldn't possibly know.

*

In the bathroom, after I have washed my face, I see Hector's razor, glinting at the edge of the sink. I pick it up, turning it over and over in my hands, looking at the faint blue lines that run under the skin of my wrist.

After standing there for some time, I put the razor back.

Lying under the sheets in the darkness, I wait for her to come to me. She doesn't, and I don't know if I am happy or sad.

Just as I am drifting off, I think I hear someone else breathing. Holding my breath, I can still hear the slow breaths like waves receding and coming back, over and over. My heart beats faster: there is something heavy on my arm. I try to lift it, and I feel her there, hear her quiet protestation. Her body is warm and I shuffle closer, cupping myself around her. The smell is unpleasant: mildew and smoke, and it makes me ache as I breathe her in, burying my face in her musty hair.

We lie together for a long time. As I reach out, stroking her hair with my fingertips, I feel her stir. Her body tenses, her hand clutching mine, squeezing it. I hear something then, the sound of something far above our heads. She squeezes my hand again, moving her narrow body closer to mine. 'He's coming,' she whispers, urgently.

I hear the door of the bedroom begin to open. Under the covers, I pull her closer. There are heavy footsteps, moving across the room; a dark shadow looms over me. I hear myself cry out and I reach to switch the bedroom light on.

But there is no one there, and she is gone. She doesn't

come back. I flick the light off and lie awake for a long time, afraid to go to sleep.

Hector comes up sometime later. I hear him, trying to be quiet. The bathroom light throws a square of yellow onto the bedroom floor before he can shut it behind him. I hear the rush of water and Hector coughing under his breath. I imagine him in front of the mirror, cupping the water in his broad hands and splashing his face.

The toilet flushes, and the door opens. He leaves it open a crack and from the bed I watch his shadow as he removes his clothes and folds them neatly onto the chair. His sagging nipples and stomach reveal themselves as he turns to the side to remove his vest. Finally, he stands in his boxer shorts removing his socks. The tufts of hair on his head are like wire wool.

He climbs into the bed, moving closer to me until I feel his arms around me, his breath on my neck, his warm stomach against my back.

*

I dream of Hector's classroom at the school across the valley. It smells of chalk and wood, and blue light streams through the huge windows which spread across the far wall.

I am standing at the back of the room, watching

Hector at the blackboard, wearing his blue jacket with patches at the elbows. He turns away from me, reaching up and writing something slowly on the blackboard. I watch the back of his head, his drooping shoulders, the awkward bend of his arm. His fingers tremble, but the letters and numbers come out clearly. He tries to explain the formula to me, but I can't work it out, however hard I try. He frowns, tutting under his breath. *You're not logical*, he says. *If you were a rational person, you would understand.*

I have failed him again.

*

Some time later, through my sleep, I hear the sounds of a man breathing. The room is totally dark, and I try and lift myself up, but there is something heavy on top of me and I can't move. The breathing is slow, and quiet. There's something in between my legs; I can feel my nightgown has ridden up. I try to pull it down, but I'm stuck, pinned to the bed. Crying out, still bleary with sleep, I push the thing away, but something takes hold of my hands.

Then I feel something between my legs, and there is a sharp pain. The breathing is getting faster. I try to push it away, but I can't.

I cry out, my voice hoarse.

The bedside light flicks on. Hector's face is over mine.

'What's the matter?' he asks.

'What are you doing?' I say.

'What do you mean?'

'You were . . . on top of me,' I say.

He looks confused. 'You woke me up,' he says.

'I was asleep,' I say.

'No, I was asleep,' he says, 'and then I felt your hands on me. I thought you wanted to.'

I sit up in bed. 'I was asleep, Hector.'

Hector shakes his head. 'That's not what happened,' he says.

His eyes are bleary from sleep, but he is sweating, the hairs on his chest damp.

We stare at each other. I slide my legs out of the bed. I feel disgusting, my skin clammy.

'Where are you going?' he says.

'To have a shower,' I say.

'It's the middle of the night, Marta.'

'Well, I'm awake now,' I say, 'and I need a shower.'

Hector sighs, and sinks back into the bed.

In the bathroom, I lean close to the mirror and tell myself that I know what happened. That I was asleep, and that it was Hector who woke me. That I am in control of my actions, that I don't sleep walk or worse. I am Marta Bjornstad, I say. If that is true, though, my husband has just tried to rape me. I'd almost rather believe that I was losing my mind.

17

I walk out of the bathroom and through the dark bedroom, past Hector's gentle snoring. Downstairs, I go to the living room. The large bay window is filled with black squares. I watch the light fixture on the ceiling until my eyes burn. Shutting my eyes, I watch the coloured dots shrink and grow. Then I do it again. And again. Soon, I can't see anything but white.

I cross the room, from one end to the other, counting my steps. Twelve steps across. I keep going. I lose count. I begin again, this time putting one foot directly in front of the other, no gap, and walking in a straight line. If I step too far, or not straight enough, I start over. I get to three hundred and fifty-seven. I stop and watch my bare feet against the carpet for a long time. Ten toes, ten toenails, ten toes, ten toenails, ten toes ten toenails ten toes ten toenails.

I go to the hall. Outside, the day is beginning, the blue light filling the hallway, making everything cold and flat.

It feels as if the light is fading, turning to darkness. I put my hands up to my temples, needing the light to come back, to make everything clear again.

Drawing the blind at the small hall window, it is still not light enough. I open it, feeling the cold air push against my cheeks, my blood rising. In the kitchen, I push back the patio doors as far as they will go. I don't stop until every curtain is pulled back, every window opened.

Still, there are shadows everywhere: behind picture frames, under furniture, at the corners of my vision.

I stand at the front door and look at the snow. The blue light makes everything glow. When I look down at the raised wooden porch, the stone doorstep has been pushed aside and there is a deep black hole.

She's lying there, her body like a child's in the white pyjamas with the pink hearts, dirty and stained yellow. This is the thinnest I have seen her. I wonder if she is dead, as I kneel down by her side, taking her hand in mine. I cup my hand over her mouth, but feel nothing. Just as I am giving up hope, I feel a slight warmth on my palm. Putting my ear down close, I hear her breath rattle in and out, in time with mine. I lie down, wrapping my body around her, rubbing her hands, trying to warm her up.

Some time later, I open my eyes. They are heavy, but

as I lift the lids a little, I make out the white pyjamas I'm wearing. My breath wheezes in and out of my chest: blinking makes me ache. When I try to move, everything is slow and heavy, as if my body is weighed down. I want to shut my eyes and go back to sleep.

Then there are hands behind my head and under my back, and I am being lifted. I try to call out, but my mouth is pressed against material. It smells familiar, and I lean closer.

I feel my head loll back, my mouth slip open. I see the blue sky above us, so huge and vast, and I blink as the sun swings across my vision. My head rings with the sharp new light. I hear a man panting. We are at the doorway, going back into the dark. I reach out for the edge of the doorframe. He stops, unhooks my hands. They fall, and then we're through the door, and he shuts it behind us.

He is breathing quickly now, as he lowers me onto the floor of the hallway. I watch his face hover over mine, shadowy in the dim hall light.

'Marta?' he says.

I blink, making out the man's features: the sagging skin around the face, the clear blue eyes. It is Hector.

I look down at my body. I am myself again. But I was her: I was in her body and it felt like there was no escape.

'What happened?' I say.

'I found you on the doorstep,' he says. It still feels eerily familiar. 'You're freezing.' He puts his warm hand onto my forehead. 'Why are all the doors and windows open?'

'You carried me in?' I ask.

'I had to. You wouldn't respond,' he says. 'I was talking to you for ages, trying to get you to wake up. I couldn't just leave you out there.'

I see the thin layer of wetness on his forehead.

'Is your knee OK?' I ask.

He shrugs. 'It'll be fine.'

'I didn't hear you,' I say.

'I know,' he says. 'I was worried about you. I am worried. You're like how you were when I first found you, Marta.' Hector's eyes are wide. 'I carried you in then, too. You were too weak to walk.'

He rubs my arms.

'You found me on the doorstep?' I say.

Hector nods. 'You were so thin and ill, like a ghost. Much easier to carry.' He smiles. 'But I couldn't leave you out there then either. I could tell you were a good person. And I was right.'

As Hector takes my hand, I see a younger Hector's face, leaning over the bath as he washed my body. Wrapping me in a towel, he sat me on the edge of the bed.

He pulled through my hair with a comb, gently at first, and then harder, until he was holding it at the roots and brushing the ends roughly. He dried it with a new hair-dryer which came from a packet: despite the warmth my teeth still chattered. Asking me to open my mouth, he checked my teeth, moving my head up and down, looking at the dark hole where one was missing. He told me we'd have to get that looked at, asked me if I could remember how it happened.

I look up at him now, trying to piece it together, but I'm so tired.

'I don't remember,' I say.

'Well, who knows what you'd been taking? You hadn't eaten in a long time by the look of you. You couldn't even feed yourself.'

He smiles. Again, I see a flash of Hector breaking biscuits between his hands and feeding them into my mouth, slowly. Then later, there was chocolate and cakes, anything to coerce me into eating. But my mouth doesn't move: anything he puts in just rolls back out again. I hear him curse.

'Let's get you warm and back to bed,' he says. 'I'll bring you a hot-water bottle. Like the old days.'

*

Hector turns on the shower and the steam starts filling the room, losing our reflections in the mirror. I am so cold. He helps me take my clothes off and then I step beneath the flow of the water. It's warm, soothing, and I start to feel better.

When I step out, Hector is gone and I am alone. Standing on the bathmat, a towel wrapped around me, I watch the steam begin to fade. There is a dark shadow next to me in the mirror. Through the misted surface, I make out her bleary reflection, coming clearer. Her hair, lacking colour, grey from the lack of sunlight. A huge matted mess, broken ends catching the light like a halo. It is the worst I have seen her look. I can make out the shape of her skull: the thin skin pulled tight, the cavernous holes under her cheek bones, the deep purple marks underneath her eyes. She is standing next to me, a skeleton covered in thin white skin.

There's someone else reflected in the mirror too, standing behind her. He is taller, wider, than her. His face is blurred, but I make out the dark hair, the broad shoulders. For a moment I think it is Kylan and I wonder what he is doing here.

'You look dreadful,' he says.

I look at her, at the colour of her skin, at how thin she is.

'I want to take care of you,' he says. 'I want to make you better.'

She doesn't smile, just stares straight ahead.

'Would you like to stay here for a while?'

She looks around her, her face turning slowly. As she looks past me, I see her pupils are huge, her eyes dead, as she looks behind her into the bedroom: the big bed that waits there, with its enormous soft duvet cover.

She nods.

He smiles, puts his hands on her shoulders. 'You must take your medicine,' he says.

In his hand, he holds a small orange pot. He opens it, dropping something into his hand. 'Open your mouth,' he says.

I see her moist pink tongue. He puts a small pink pill into her mouth and she swallows it without any water.

'Good girl,' he says, putting his hand on her head.

I turn around, wanting to see his face, but I am too late – he's gone.

I look back at the mirror. Marta stands there, alone, a towel wrapped around her body. Her lined face stares back at me, her grey eyes wide.

*

Once I am in bed, Hector comes up. I try to lift myself, but he is sitting on my legs. He has a tray on his knees and uses his long nails to flip open the top of the Tupperware box resting on it, condensation clouding the lid.

There is a sharp smell of fish. I watch Hector spoon the food out into a bowl. He ladles some of it onto a spoon, and lifts it towards my mouth.

'I can do it, Hector,' I say, trying to sit up again, but he fills my mouth with food so I can't speak any more. He continues to feed me until the bowl is empty.

'Now, I don't mind taking care of you,' he says. 'But I think we should go and see someone next week when you're feeling up to it. It looks like your pills have stopped working, and we might need to try something new.'

'Hector, I'm fine—'

He holds his hand up.

'Marta, we both know that isn't true. You need to get some help. It's nothing to be ashamed of.'

I stare at him.

'Kylan's really worried about you,' he says.

'I think I might just be remembering things,' I say, 'from when I first came to live with you. I don't think I need any more medication.'

'I don't understand why you want to remember those

things, Marta,' he says, putting his hand on the crown of my head. 'You weren't yourself back then.'

'I think I need to.'

'It's much better if you just take your pills,' he says. 'We'll find you some new ones that work better. You've got past all that.'

'Maybe I haven't,' I say. 'Maybe that's why I need to remember.'

I still can't sit up properly, so I can't look him in the eye. He squeezes my hand.

'I'm your husband, Marta,' he says. 'I know what's best for you. It can't do you any good to put yourself through all this. It's not rational. We'll go and see Thomas again. See if he can't prescribe something new.'

And then it flashes before my eyes: shivering in the draughty waiting room, Hector's hand over mine. The man from the pub with the beery breath, leaning over me. The doctor. The rumble of Hector's voice. *I found her, Thomas. She hasn't been eating.* Thomas nods. *She hasn't spoken, but she cries in her sleep about her parents.* The doctor's hands are cold.

I can tell he is never going to understand, so I nod.

'Good girl,' he says. 'Now get some rest.'

'Are you going to stay here?' I ask.

'I might pop out and see Mother later,' he says. 'But

you don't need to come. Stay here, where it's safe.' He strokes my cheek. 'I hope you feel better soon, darling.'

He bends down, kisses me on the forehead, and then leaves the room.

18

I lie awake, listening for him in the house. I don't want to be in bed: I want to get up, to walk around the house and think. The stories Hector has told me about what happened before we got married don't quite feel right. Now that the darker side of things has shown itself, it's not easy to forget.

Eventually, after what feels like hours, I hear the front door slam. Going to the window, I watch Hector, in his big coat and gloves: putting on the snow chains, de-icing the windscreen. He looks up at the house and I duck down behind the curtain. I listen to the engine start up, peering out again, watching the grey car move slowly down the lane and out of sight.

I go straight to Hector's study, lifting paper after paper on his desk. I read all the postcards on the notice board, and then I start on the drawers. Stationery supplies, folders, paperclips: nothing is amiss. Examining the bookshelf, the books are boring, with titles I don't understand, and when I pull them down the pages inside are written in symbols, utterly incomprehensible.

Then I see it, on the second shelf: *How To Be a Good Wife*. I pull it down, and flick through the pages, but it is all familiar: crude drawings and photos of grinning women doing domestic tasks, and the accompanying tips. There is nothing here I haven't seen a million times before.

I sink back into the desk chair. Perhaps Hector is right. Perhaps the girl is only in my imagination, a part of the old me that I am better off forgetting. I have a good life here, with a loving husband and son, and there are lots of things to look forward to. There is the wedding, and watching Kylan's life unfold. Grandchildren. Perhaps we could even move closer to the city.

When I look up, I see her feet, clad in ballet shoes, the ribbons trailing across the floor. Pink legs, tights, muscular thighs, and her leotard. She has her hands on her hips, her hair scraped into a bun. Her face is made up, and she wears black eyeliner underneath her wide grey eyes. She reaches out for my hand. I take it and pull myself to my feet.

On unsteady legs, I follow her along the corridor, down the stairs, through the hallway. She opens the front door and steps out, pulling me after her. It is cold; the valley is still and white. She lets go of my hand, kneels down next to the huge slab of stone that is the porch step, and begins to push at it, motioning for me to help her. We push and push until it begins to move. That sound: of stone on stone, of the earth shifting. I feel my teeth clench, my muscles ache. I let out a noise of frustration, but it's moving now, out of the way. I keep pushing. A dark space emerges, as long as the porch step and just wide enough to fit through. I peer into a low crawl space, running underneath the house, about a metre high. The daylight reveals the ends of two poles, like broomsticks, jammed horizontally into the space that must run underneath the hole. I pull and the edge of a ladder emerges.

I sit up and look at her. She nods. Getting up, I go back into the house and get the torch we keep under the kitchen sink, for emergencies. When I return to the hole, she is gone.

I look around me at the long empty stretch of our driveway. The sky spreads out above me, and I can hear the sounds of birdsong nearby. The sun shines: it is a crisp cold day full of air that feels brand new. The lane is empty, the valley deserted. No one can see me here.

Lowering myself into the space, there is a narrow earthy area, only about a metre across, in which I can just crouch. As my eyes adjust to the light, I make it out:

a metal door in a metal frame dug into the earth at my feet. I push on the door, expecting it to be locked, but it opens a fraction. All is dark below. Pushing again, the metal jarring, it moves a bit further, then more, until it is fully open.

I clap my hand over my mouth: the smell coming from the hole is strong and I can't bear it. Mildew, mould and something else, some sad smell that makes my toes curl.

Shining the torch, I make out a small room, two metres square, two metres deep. The narrow beam of white light flashes over the shadowed frame of an old bed, not big enough, with a thin mattress. There is a duvet cover, bunched into a pile. A table, grimy with dust after all these years, blotches rising from the surface. A toilet with no lid, its dark mouth disappearing into the shadows. There is a sponge in the sink in the corner, a nub of soap. The yellow clock with its grinning black face is on the wall, long stopped, the hands marking ten minutes past three.

I move the light back to the bed and see her sitting there, on the pillow, with her back against the concrete wall and her legs crossed. She holds a fan of cards in her hands, jiggling her legs, and reaches forward to pick up a card from the pile.

He is sitting opposite her with his back to me. His hair is brown. I watch him reach his hand forward and pick up a card, his nails long for a man.

'Gin rummy,' he says.

She tuts. 'I only need one more card.'

He lays out his cards into two piles on the duvet cover. 'Sorry,' he says. He scoops them up.

She keeps her cards in her hand.

He reaches for them.

She moves them out of the way. 'Are you going now?' she says.

'In a minute.'

'We haven't played chess yet,' she says.

'We'll have to play another day.'

He tries to hand the cards to her, but she won't take them so he puts them on the duvet. 'I'll try and come back soon,' he says, still sitting.

He watches as she picks up the cards and starts to lay them out.

'There's something I need to tell you,' he says.

She looks up.

He pulls out a piece of paper from his pocket and hands it to her.

I watch the colour drain from her face, her mouth drop open.

'Where did you get this picture?' she says, her voice breathy, thick, like fog.

'The newspaper,' he says.

I watch her run the tip of her finger over the small square of paper, murmur something inaudible under her breath. She looks up at him.

'How did you know that they are my—'

'I'm afraid they're dead,' he says, speaking over her.

Her face changes, wiped blank. Her eyes turn black.

'There was a car accident.'

She shakes her head. 'I don't believe you,' she says.

'I'm sorry,' he says. 'But it's true. I thought you should know.'

She still stares. He stands up and I can see the top of his head. Quickly, she folds the picture up and slides it under the mattress.

He props the ladder into place.

'I'll try and come back soon,' he says.

He puts one foot on the bottom rung, and I switch off the torch and sink further into the crawl space. When he reaches the top, he pauses, as if he has heard something. He turns and looks right at me, his clear blue eyes all I can make out in the darkness. I look back at him, but his eyes register nothing.

It's Hector, as I knew it would be. It has been Hector all along.

I lean forward, ready to push him back into the darkness, to pull the heavy door shut and lock him down there, but when I switch on the torch again, they are gone. The bed is empty, the duvet a messy pile again, the smell still overwhelming. Quickly, I lift the ladder back into place, and holding my breath, climb down into the room. I reach down to the bed frame, feeling under the mattress. The edge of the newspaper cutting meets my fingers. I lift it out, clambering back up the ladder. Slamming the door down, I climb out of the crawl space. I blink in the sunshine, try to dust some of the dirt off the front of my nightgown.

In the kitchen, I lean over the sink. A mess of hot brown emerges from my mouth; my stomach burns. I stare at the smear in the glancing silver of the sink bowl: it begins to swim before my eyes. My heart is thumping hard, sending shooting pains through my chest. I clutch the edge of the kitchen surface. I can't breathe: my breaths trip over each other, coming faster, each one shallower than the last. Finding my way to a kitchen chair, I sit down and put my head in my hands. I can feel the blood in my temples. I try to count the beats, but they slip past me, faster and faster.

I open the piece of folded paper in my hand. It's small and square, cut from the newspaper, nothing but a picture with text on the back from some other story. A man and a woman stand under a tree in a garden. The man has a slight smile at the corner of his mouth, and in a rush, I feel his hand on my shoulder, the smell of leather and Paco Rabanne, so strong I almost cry out. The woman has long dark-blonde hair, almost down to her slight waist, and I feel it brushing against my cheek as she leans down to give me a kiss goodnight. In between them stands a girl with blonde hair, squinting into the sunlight. It is her. It is me.

I need to get out of here. Telling myself I will look at it again later, I climb the stairs two at a time. In our bedroom, I pull off my nightgown and dress in jeans and a black polo neck. I don't bother with underwear. Slipping the piece of newspaper into my pocket, I reach into the bottom of our shared wardrobe and pull out the old green overnight bag. I throw things in, as much as I can, until it is full. I raid the bathroom: toothbrush, toothpaste, soap, towel. Taking my jewellery out of the top drawer of my dresser, I collect my make-up and a picture of Kylan that lives there. I pull at the zip, willing it to close.

Downstairs, I stop in the hallway, trying to think clearly if there is anything else I need. Looking down at my shaking hands, I see my wedding ring, glinting against the strap of the bag. I pull it off and drop it onto the kitchen table.

As I walk back through the hallway, I see the huge cabinet on the wall, crammed with the frozen faces of my dolls. I walk to the doors, open them, and pull out my favourite doll: the one with the white blonde hair and grey eyes. Peeling off her pink dress, I hold her naked body in the palms of my hands. Turning her over, I slam her into the wall next to the cabinet, over and over, as hard as I can. I hear a crack. I keep going. Then I put her back into the cabinet.

Opening the front door, the large stone doorstep is where I left it, exposing a dark opening. There is no time to lose. I lean forward and push the stone back into place, sweat breaking across my forehead, tears springing into my eyes in frustration. When it looks like it always has, I get up and go to the other car.

I throw the bag into the boot and open the driver's door. I hear a vehicle approaching. Through the windscreen, I can see the tight line of Hector's mouth, his eyes concentrating on the road ahead. He raises his hand in a wave.

I stay where I am.

He pulls into the drive, pauses for a moment and rolls down the window, blocking my way.

'On your way out?' he says.

'I need to get a few things from town.' I feel my voice tremble.

'Are you feeling better?' he says.

I smile. 'Much,' I say.

His brow wrinkles. 'Are you sure you're OK to go out?'

I nod. 'Can you make me an appointment to see a doctor next week?'

Hector's eyebrows rise.

'I think you're right,' I say. 'We need to put this all behind us.'

He smiles. 'How long will you be?'

'An hour, two at the most.'

'If you wait a minute, I'll come,' he says.

I look at my watch. It is almost one o'clock. 'I want to catch the market before they pack up,' I say. 'I won't be long.'

My heart shudders in my chest.

'I'll see you later.'

He rolls the window back up, pulls forward into the drive. Pulling out onto the road, I turn left, away from town, pressing my foot down on the accelerator.

19

I drive fast, passing the pale blue farmhouse, the yard scattered with junk and scrap metal, the sign advertising eggs that nobody ever sees. The red buildings lie low in the valley; the machinery waits.

Speeding through a tunnel of green-and-white trees, I check the rear-view mirror repeatedly. The road behind me is empty. Turning left, I begin the zigzagged incline, traversing the mountain, making my way out of the valley. It slopes upwards, disappearing into dark carved rock tunnels and then re-emerging into the white world. To my left, I can see the patches of snow clinging to the land below; the vast stretch of water glimmers through the morning haze. I imagine my little car tumbling down the side of the mountain and into the water, filling slowly but surely, sinking below the surface.

At the top, the next valley is laid out before me. The sharp, rocky crags; the new fjord, a silvered mass like the belly of a fish. I have never seen this side of the mountains, and I feel a thrill run through me like an un-coiling ribbon.

There are hikers here, their tight, strong bodies wrapped in walking clothes: scarves and hats and gloves. My eye is drawn to a man and a girl, hand in hand. The man is tall and thin with sandy blond hair, and the girl's white blonde hair is plaited. He smiles as I drive past, and I feel an ache of familiarity. When I glance in the rear-view mirror, they have disappeared.

As I look for them, the smell of boiled sweets and wet canvas fills the car. I hear music, too-loud rock. I feel a sweet wrapper beneath my fingers, the wetness of his mouth as I drop it in. His golden hair shining in the orange evening sun; stubby fingernails tapping the steer-ing wheel along with the music. The sound of the wind flapping against the tent, green morning light through the material. Then it's gone again, and I am alone, driving down a steep road, moving faster and faster. I put my foot on the brake, straightening the steering wheel. When the road flattens out, I come to a passing place and pull the car over.

I slip the scrap of newspaper out of my pocket and hold it up to the light. It is a black-and-white photo-graph, grainy, soft and malleable in my hands.

We are standing in front of the wide dark spruce tree

which grows in the garden. Its shadow falls behind us, heightening the brightness of the sun which reflects our skin.

My father stands proud under the lower branches of the tree. His sandy hair falls neatly down the centre of his head. I see a flash then, of the evening light in his hair, and I know it was him in the car with me.

My mother stands next to him, smiling widely at the camera, her arm around my father's waist. Her dark blonde hair falls over her shoulders and she wears a summer dress I remember with red cherries on the front, her feet bare. She looks impossibly young.

I stand in front of my parents, wearing a dress with puffy sleeves and flowers across the bottom. My hair is pulled back, and the sunlight wipes out everything except for a mouth and two dim black holes for eyes. I remember the itch of the dress at my neck: how hot it was, standing in the sun.

Looking up, I find myself at the side of the road. I know I don't have long. Once Hector sees the empty wardrobe, my wedding ring on the kitchen table, I'm sure he will be right behind me, driving fast. I run my fingers over the different faces, breathing them in. Remembering.

*

I drive through villages and towns. Even out here, there are road signs that point the way towards the city and I follow them. The sun shines from the roofs of the wooden houses along the roadside. After a while each conglomeration of village necessities, village shop, pub, the older magnificence of the hotels, starts to blend together into one long unchanging stretch of green. I pass glassy fjords that reflect the huge sky: my head soars. I have always known it was a long way.

I have broken the rules. *You are not to go further than here. It is not safe.* I hear Hector's voice, filling the car, and then I am in the passenger seat, bundled in a heap of blankets. The sound of the engine, musty and loud: the rattle of warm air through the vents. Outside the window, the greens moved too fast, the mountains loomed too large, and I shut my eyes, resting my head against his shoulder. Through his chest, I heard the rumbling of his voice as he pointed out the town hall, the post office, the hotels. At the school, he stopped the car.

'When you are on your own,' he said, 'this is as far as you are to go. You are never to leave the valley.'

I lifted my head up. 'I don't want to be on my own,' I said.

He smiled. 'Don't look so frightened,' he said. 'I only mean later, when you are feeling better.'

I put my head back on his shoulder.

'I'll always be here,' he said.

*

When I reach the outskirts of the city, it's night time. The clock reads 21:55. In the dark, it is harder to watch out for Hector. The road has widened out and there are many more cars now, speeding past and cutting in front, their lights glaring.

Grey industrial buildings and long shop warehouses line the road, their brightly lit signs offering computers, fitness equipment, electrical appliances. Reaching a round-about, I circle it three times before I remember the way. I pass a tall white block of flats, and then I am in the city streets. There are so many houses, so many people.

Wide old trees stand at the roadside, their few shadowy leaves shuddering in the evening wind. There is a huge brick building with a flag on a long white pole outside. The terraced town houses, lit up inside, look familiar. Even in the darkness, it is as if nothing has changed, like seeing a forbidden old friend again. I am sure that the answers are waiting here, and I am glad I came back.

Stopping at a red light, my leg begins to shake on the accelerator. There is a crowd of people standing at a bus stop, huddled together in the cold. As the lights turn green and I start to move off, I see a girl wearing a red coat, a sports bag slung over her shoulder. Under the street lamp, her blonde hair glows.

I slam the brakes on, ignoring the blasts of horns from the cars behind me. My heart beats faster. There are no other people at the bus stop now, no cars on the road, only her. She looks down the street, both ways. I can tell she is worried, and as she turns her back, I see a pink ribbon escaping from her bag, caught in the zip, the end fluttering in the wind.

She rocks back and forward on her heels, wraps her arms around herself, rubs her shoulders. Her breath leaves a misty trail, making it hard to see her face. She slides a box out of her pocket, slipping out a cigarette, white as bone.

Then I see the car, driving along the road towards her. It slows as it approaches the bus stop, and the window begins to wind down. She leans, her blonde hair falling forward. She shakes her head, and I see her smiling. I watch her lips move. *No, thank you.* Then she stops. She shrugs, drops her cigarette onto the floor, opens the car door, and slides in. The door shuts and they drive on, disappearing into the darkness.

The cars are zooming past me now. Some beep their horns, some don't, but I can barely hear them. I sit and stare at the bus stop for a long time. I remember coveting that red coat in the window of a department store, buying it once I had saved up. It was the first thing I bought for myself, with my own money, won in competitions. My mother told me the sleeves were too short, that I should have got a bigger size, and I was annoyed with her. I feel the cold air against my cheeks on the walk to the bus stop that evening. Another night practising late and things hadn't gone well, and now I had missed the last bus. I didn't want to call my parents: I was still annoyed with my mother. Then the car pulled in, and the man inside offered to give me a lift. He was older, and he looked concerned, his blue eyes clear and unsettled: he reminded me of my father. He didn't look like he would harm anyone, so I climbed in, and told him my address. He nodded. He drove at a normal speed, in the right direction.

'What are you doing out so late?' he said.

It was nearly ten o'clock. 'I had ballet class,' I said.

'Ballet?' he asked. 'What kind of a studio is open at this time?'

I smiled. 'I have a key.'

'I was worried about a young girl like you, out so late,' he said. 'You should be careful.'

I shrugged. 'I always catch the bus home about this time,' I say. 'Except tonight I was a little late.'

'Lucky I was passing,' he said.

We were heading into my suburb now, and I began to relax, to think about making some cheese on toast when

I got home. The man handed me an open bottle of something which smelled like aquavit.

'Would you like some?' he said.

We were close to my road now: only a few moments, and we would be pulling up in front of my house. I liked the idea of my mother smelling the alcohol on my breath, of her wondering what I had been up to. I took a big swig from the bottle.

The man smiled. 'I would join you,' he said. 'But I don't like to drink and drive. I wouldn't want to get pulled over.'

The low lights of the familiar houses flashed past as we circled my neighbourhood. As we approached the turning for my road, he didn't slow down.

'That was it,' I said, my voice strangely thick.

The man didn't seem to hear me.

'It was back there,' I said again.

I remember the outline of his nose, his tight lips against the suburban lights: his hands clenching the steering wheel. Then all around me the world began to fade, dimming like the failing light of winter, until everything was dark.

20

I have to pull over and check the address several times, but eventually I find the road and park the car.

Carrying my bag, I walk along the street until I reach the right number. The building is the only red one in a long row of terraced houses. A low black fence runs along the front. I open the gate, walk up three stone steps, and press the buzzer for Flat 3.

'Hello?'

'Kylan?' I say. 'It's your mother. Can you let me up?'

I hear the buzz of the door opening. When I reach the top of the stairs, he's standing at the door.

'Hi, darling,' I say, reaching forward to give him a hug.

He stops me. 'Mum, have you been crying?' he says.

'I'm fine,' I say.

He hugs me then, and stands aside so I can walk in. The walls are painted red and the floors are wooden. I follow Kylan down the corridor and through a door.

It's a small kitchen with a generous window on the far wall, through which I can see the lights of the street below.

Kylan gestures to a chair at the table and I sit down.

'I thought you'd be more surprised to see me,' I say.

'Dad rang,' he says. 'He said you might turn up.' He steps over to the kitchen counter, flicking the switch on the side of the kettle. 'Tea?'

I nod. 'What did he say?' I ask.

'He was worried,' he says, reaching into a cupboard for some mugs. 'Said you'd gone out to the shops and hadn't come back. He found your wedding ring on the kitchen table and most of your clothes were gone.'

He puts a mug of tea in front of me and sits down.

'What's going on, Mum?'

'There's something I need to tell you,' I say. 'Something about your father.'

He blows on his tea, his sandy hair falling messily across his forehead. I remember a picture he drew when he was a little boy: a man and a woman with their arms around each other and a little boy standing in the middle. I hear Kylan and Hector laughing from the other side of the study door.

I wonder how to continue. 'He's not—' I start. 'He's not who I thought he was.'

'What do you mean?'

'Things haven't been easy.' This is impossible. 'I'm going to go to the police,' I say. 'Tomorrow. But I wanted to talk to you first.'

Kylan's eyes widen. 'The police? Why would you need to go to the police?'

'I've stopped taking my pills and I've started remembering things,' I say. 'Your father made me take them.' I pause, trying to find the right words. 'He's a bad man.'

Kylan is staring at me, the line between his eyes deepening. 'Mum, I don't understand what you're saying,' he says. 'What has Dad done?'

'For a long time, I couldn't remember where your father and I met.' I laugh. 'Isn't that strange? He always says we met on holiday, and I could remember being there with him, but I didn't remember meeting him there. I remembered him taking care of me, after my parents died.'

'There are photos of you,' he says. 'On the island. Sitting at a restaurant by the water. Your first date.'

'But I've started remembering things before that,' I say. 'I never chose him, not how you chose Katya. He chose me.'

He's staring at me blankly. 'Mum. I don't understand. What are you saying?'

'He said he found me on the doorstep,' I say, slowly. 'That I was ill. But I think he made me like that.'

'Like what?'

'He made me ill. He told me there was a car crash, but it isn't true. He told you that too. I'm so sorry, Kylan.'

I start to cry then. Kylan doesn't come and put his arm around me. He sits across the table and stares.

'Perhaps we should talk about it in the morning,' he says. 'You're obviously very tired.'

I grasp his hand. 'I don't want to tell you this,' I say, the tears coming again. Since they started at the bus stop, I can't seem to stop them. 'I'm not even sure if I'm right. Perhaps I should be taking my pills.'

'Why have you stopped taking them?'

'I suppose I wanted to see what would happen,' I say.

'But you know what happens. You've done it before.'

'I wanted to know what I was like without them,' I say. 'And I'm starting to think that maybe they've been stopping me from remembering things.'

Kylan gets up, puts his arm around me, pulls me to my feet. 'Come on, Mum,' he says. 'We can talk about it all in the morning.'

I grab hold of his arm. 'I need you to help me, Kylan,' I say. 'I need to figure it out.'

Kylan stares at me. 'Figure what out?'

'What really happened.'

'I'll help you as much as I can,' he says. 'But I think you should get some sleep. It might feel different in the morning.'

I let him lead me down the corridor and into a small square room with just enough room for a double bed. There is a dresser squeezed in alongside it, with a pot of dried lavender on the top.

'Is Katya here?'

'She's gone to bed. Do you want me to get you anything?'

'I'll be fine,' I say, sitting on the edge of the bed. He stays standing there, as if unsure what to do next.

'Well, the bathroom's at the end of the hall,' he says. He turns to leave.

'Kylan,' I say. He stops in the doorway and turns back. 'I'm so sorry.'

'What for?' he says.

'Just please don't tell him I'm here.'

Kylan looks at me for a moment, and then leaves the room.

*

I dream of the blonde girl.

Smiling, she dodges me, and I see her running across

a beach. She doesn't look back, but I can hear her laughing. She is young; the sunlight glances off her still-blonde hair. All is light there: it shines on her and from her.

It's warmer where she is. I can tell by the way her image shimmers and blurs at the edges. It is where I would be now. If, if, if.

Finally, I catch up with her. She's trying to tell me something: I watch her mouth move, hear the sounds, but I can't make out the word she is saying.

She splashes into the sea and plunges underwater, her body like an arcing seal. Rushing into the water, I swim deeper and deeper, my eyes stinging with salt. I force them open. I swim for a long time, but I can't find her. When I return to the surface, I look down at my body, touch my blonde hair. It is hers. I have found her at last.

The word is on my lips when I wake up.

Elise.

21

The first thing I see when I open my eyes is Kylan. He's sitting on the edge of the bed wearing a red dressing gown. He smiles at me, a tight, wary smile. For a moment, I see him as a little boy again, his hair pushed up away from his forehead, messy with sleep.

'Morning,' he says. 'Did you sleep well?'

'Yes.' I remember Hector and look at the door.

'He's not here, Mum,' he says. 'I told him not to come.'

'Did he call?'

'I called him,' he says. 'I've taken the day off work today. I thought we could spend it together.'

'Where's Katya?'

'She's gone to work,' he says. 'It's just you and me.'

I smile then, embarrassed to feel the tears rise. With difficulty, I bring my eyes up to his. They are clear and blue. 'I'm sorry, Mum,' he says, his voice breaking. 'I didn't realize things were so bad with you.' He pauses. 'I should have done more to help.'

'I'm fine now,' I say, looking around the clean, white room. 'I'm safe here.'

Kylan looks uneasy. 'You're safe at home, Mum.'

'Don't make me go back there, Kylan,' I say.

He is looking at my hands and looking down I see I'm clutching the duvet cover, both fists tight.

'Let's get dressed and go out for breakfast,' he says. 'There's a cafe nearby that Katya and I like.'

I let my hands relax and try to smile. 'You have the first shower,' I say.

*

We leave the house at quarter past ten.

The sunlight bounces off the tall row of terraced houses opposite, the different colours melding brightly together like rock candy. For a second, I feel a sweet stickiness between my teeth: hear the roar of waves, the sound of seagulls. Then there is the smell of the sea. I shut my eyes, trying to draw the memory out, but just as quickly as it came, it's gone again.

There are people in the street, going about their daily business. The shopkeeper across the road is standing outside his shop smoking a cigarette. I feel the smoke filling my own lungs, the cigarette shaking between my fingers.

'Mum?'

Kylan is ahead, waiting for me. I must have stopped walking. It is as if the city itself is trying to help me, dropping clues which are impossible to ignore.

After a while, we come to a cafe, and Kylan holds the door open for me. Inside, it's warm and smells of frying bacon. There are wooden tables and a blackboard above the counter announcing the menu in spindly white letters.

I follow him to a table. A red-headed waitress comes over, and we order coffees.

'This is nice,' I say, smiling at him.

'Yes,' he says, looking around the room. 'We come here most Sundays for breakfast.'

I look around at the dusty wooden floors.

'What's it like being back in the city? You grew up here, right?' Kylan asks.

'I've always been so worried about coming back here,' I say. 'Your father told me so often it was bad for me.'

'I'm glad you've come,' he says. 'It's strange you've never seen my house, my life here.'

'I wanted to, Kylan,' I say. 'Your father wouldn't let me. I'm so glad I'm here now.'

Kylan smiles. 'I don't think Dad would have minded.'

'He told me I was only safe in the valley,' I say. 'But he didn't want me to remember. He knew it would be easier to remember here.'

'He just cares about you, Mum. He wants to protect you.'

'He's scared that someone will find out what he did,' I say.

'What do you think he's done, Mum?'

I take hold of Kylan's hands across the table.

'Kylan, I know this isn't easy to hear, but I don't think I can live with your father any more. I need to be far away from him.'

'I don't understand what's changed,' he says.

'I told you,' I say. 'I've started remembering things since I stopped taking my pills.'

Kylan squeezes my hand. 'Mum, I remember what you were like when you stopped taking your pills before. You weren't yourself. You were seeing things, hallucinating. I think you need to start taking them again.'

'Maybe I need to remember these things, Kylan,' I say. 'It's important.'

'But what if you're not remembering?' he says. 'What if your mind is playing tricks on you?'

'I need to be able to trust myself,' I say.

'All I'm asking is that you think about it. About taking your pills again.'

'I just need a bit of time to think things through,' I say.

The girl arrives with our coffees and we sip them in silence. I think of the wide bright streets outside the window, the colourful buildings. I think of a life without Hector.

'Perhaps I'll move back here,' I say.

Kylan stares at me.

'I could get a little apartment here, near you. Get a job in a shop or something.'

'But, Mum—' He stops. 'What about Dad?'

'Perhaps I could stay with you,' I say. 'Until I get on my feet. You have that spare room after all.'

Kylan looks away, sips his coffee. 'We'll see,' he says. 'Just think about what I've said.'

'Where are you going?' I ask, as he stands up.

'Mum, don't look so worried. I'm just going to the toilet.'

Kylan starts to walk away. I want to stop him: I hold my breath until he is gone. Then I look around the cafe. There is only one other table occupied, taken by two well-dressed women in their mid-forties. They talk and smile. I long to hear what they are saying over the sound of the coffee grinder.

I look down at the table. It has changed: it's white Formica now, with a solid metal rim. Beneath it are my legs, pink and opaque, the contours of the muscles visible through the material of my tights. I am still wearing my ballet shoes and leotard under my coat. In front of me is the biggest bowl of ice cream I've ever seen. There are several different flavours, piled high, covered with hundreds and thousands and lashings of chocolate and strawberry sauce.

I can smell something sweet, but it isn't the ice cream, it's something else, something that makes my heart beat faster. It's my mother's smell, her perfume: sweet rose water. I can see the round purple bottle on her dressing table, catching the light from the window. I look up, and she's there, sitting opposite me. She smiles, revealing the gap between her front teeth, her long ash-blonde hair slipping out from behind her ear and falling forwards. She is wearing her pale pink lipstick, and her favourite cream jumper with the trail of pink flowers at the shoulder. I remember the softness of it, and I long to reach forward and touch it.

'Aren't you going to eat that?' she says.

I dig my spoon into the edge of the mountain. The taste of vanilla fills my mouth. I eat faster, unable to stop.

She is smiling, watching me eat. I think of the ballet studio, the smell of waxed floors and cleaning product, the wide clear mirrors that spread across one wall. I see my body, moving across the floor, the delicate, floating movements of my arms and legs. And behind me, I see the rows and rows of chairs that had been set up for the competition, the faces of the audience. She was there, in the front row, grinning at me. I remember the sounds of applause; the feeling of the cool metal of the medal between my fingers.

'I'm so proud of you, Elise,' she says.

I look up, and she is gone. Kylan is sitting across from me in the cafe.

'You were miles away,' Kylan says.

'Are you done with your coffee?' I say. 'I think I'd like to get my hair cut.'

22

The salon is sleek, so different to the one in the village with its black-and-white-tile floor, blue walls, and bulky old-fashioned equipment. The willowy receptionist tells me they can see me straight away, and I am ushered through to have my hair washed before I can even think about it. As I slip my arms into the grey gown, I make Kylan promise to wait where I can see him.

The hairdresser, a petite girl with dark curly hair and big brown eyes, wraps a towel around my head and leads me to a chair facing a row of mirrors. I keep my eyes averted, not wanting to look at myself. I don't feel like the old me any more, and I don't want to look like her either.

'I want to go blonde,' I say.

She frowns. 'Your hair is blonde,' she says.

'It's too dark,' I say. 'I want to go lighter. As light as possible.'

'So you are an ash tone now, quite dark. It might be hard to go light all in one go.'

'I want it as light as you can get it.'

'And the cut?' she asks.

I reach into my pocket and slide out the old black-and-white newspaper cutting.

'Like this,' I say, pointing at Elise's face.

She squints at the picture, then looks at me. 'I can't really see the style there—'

'I want to look like that,' I say.

She looks at the picture again. Finally, she nods. I smile.

I ask her if she will cover the mirror.

She looks confused.

'Just cover the mirror with a towel or something. I don't want to see it until it is done.'

She returns with a huge white towel which she throws over the mirror. I can feel the woman in the next chair staring at me.

When she starts to cut, I watch the strands of dark wet hair drop to the ground, and I smile. I feel the heat of the hairdryer on my scalp and turn around to check on Kylan: he is sitting in the corner of the room, reading a magazine, looking bored.

She turns off the hairdryer. 'Shall I take off the towel now?' she asks.

I put my hands up, feeling the soft hair between my fingers. 'Yes,' I say.

She pulls the towel away. Behind it is a woman with blonde hair just above her shoulders, with a sweeping side fringe. I turn my head to the side. It is really her, as she would have been. I smile and she smiles back.

'It's perfect,' I say. 'Thank you.'

Kylan doesn't recognize me until I am standing right in front of him. 'Wow, Mum,' he says. 'You look so different.'

I pay with Hector's credit card, and as we leave the shop, I take Kylan's arm. It is sunny outside, bright after the dim salon, and as we walk I feel light, free. I chatter away to Kylan about how lovely the neighbourhood is around here, how nice it would be to take one of those flats with a little balcony overlooking the street. I tell him I want to live in a brightly coloured building, with lots of sunlight. Kylan lets me talk.

I stop walking. Just ahead, I see him, the back of his head disappearing around the corner. He has the same broad shoulders, the same way of walking. He holds her hand: her blonde hair moving in the breeze, her skinny body shrouded in clothes that are too big for her. He pulls her around the corner and out of sight, and as they disappear she turns, looking back over her shoulder, her huge grey eyes so wide with fear that I hear myself cry out.

I let go of Kylan's arm and find myself running.

Rounding the bend, I see them, a little way ahead. He is dragging her along, muttering under his breath for her to hurry up. I lunge forward, grasping hold of her arm and pulling her backwards. He stops, startled, and for a split second he releases her hand. I pull her after me, but she won't come. Pulling harder, I start to run, back the way I have come. 'It's all right,' I say, 'you're safe now.'

After a few minutes, I feel someone catch hold of my arm. I wrench it free and keep going. Glancing behind me, I see it is Kylan and I shout at him to stop the man from following us. He calls something back, but I keep running down the street, panting, dodging people in the way. The girl is screaming now too, crying out. 'It's all right,' I say again. 'Don't worry.'

Kylan catches up with me, taking hold of my arms.

'Mum, stop, please!' he says.

I try to pull away. 'I can't, Kylan, I need to get her to a safe place. He's coming.'

A man in his mid-thirties with messy dark brown hair runs up to us, sweating.

'Mum, just put the girl down,' Kylan says.

'We need to keep going.'

She is twisting her narrow body, stretching out her arms towards the man with the dark hair. 'Daddy,' she cries out.

'Ssh,' I say. 'That's not your daddy. I'll take you home now.'

I reach down to stroke her hair, then stop. I am holding onto the arm of a little girl, with short brown hair, her cheeks bleary with tears. Kylan moves in and takes her.

'Mum, what are you doing? She could have been hurt.'

He leads the little girl back to her father, who strokes her hair and kisses her forehead. His face is red as he swings around towards us.

'You're lucky I don't call the police,' he says.

'I know, I'm very sorry. She's not feeling herself,' Kylan says.

Kylan turns to me.

'Where is she?' I ask.

'Who?'

'There was a blonde girl with grey eyes. She's very thin.'

'I don't know what you're talking about,' he says. He looks at the crowd that has formed, at all the people staring at me. 'Let's get you home.'

'I can't go home, Kylan,' I say. 'I need to find her.' I look at the sea of faces, the open mouths and cupped hands, the whispers. 'Where is she?'

Kylan puts his arm around me, leaning close to my ear. 'Please, Mum,' he says. 'Let's go back to my house.'

I look up at him. 'She's gone now,' I say. 'He's got her again.'

*

We don't speak on the way back. By the time we get back, the streets are dark: it is almost six o'clock. The people seem fervent, hurrying. We walk for what feels like hours, until finally we reach Kylan's apartment.

As he's opening the door, I reach out and squeeze his arm.

'I'm sorry, Kylan,' I say. 'Please don't be angry with me.'

Kylan looks back at me for a moment and he looks so desperately sad and tired.

'I'm not, Mum,' he says. 'That little girl was just so frightened,' he says. 'Her father thought you were trying to take her.'

I stare at him. 'I would never do that, Kylan,' I say. 'You know that. Don't you?'

Kylan puts his hand over mine. 'Yes,' he says, then heads down the narrow hallway. I follow him up the stairs and into the warm apartment. He drops his keys onto the hall table and walks through into the kitchen.

Katya is sitting at the table eating a bowl of cereal, her feet pulled up under her.

'Hi,' she says. Kylan walks over and kisses the top of her head. I look away. 'Your hair looks nice, Mrs Bjornstad.'

I feel myself bristle at the name, putting my hand up to my hair. I had forgotten about it.

'Did you have a nice day?' she says.

Katya and Kylan exchange glances. 'It was interesting,' Kylan says. 'We had a nice coffee this morning at that cafe.'

'I think I might go to bed,' I say. 'I feel a bit ill.'

'Don't you want any supper?' she asks.

'I'm not hungry,' I say. I turn to leave the room.

'Night, Mum,' Kylan says. 'I hope you feel better soon.'

*

In the bedroom, I don't get ready for bed.

I pace, imagining Kylan telling Katya what just happened with the little girl. I know what it must have looked like, and it will sound even worse. I saw Kylan's face in the cafe when I tried to explain things to him. Of course he doesn't want to see his father as anything but a good man.

I find a pad of paper and a pen on the bedside table. Sitting on the edge of the bed, I decide to write down everything I know.

I write the word *Elise*. I can't remember a surname.

Below it, *Ballet. Studio. Wooden floors, smell of cleaner, mirrors along one side*.

It could be any ballet studio anywhere. Squeezing my eyes shut, I try to see the outside of the building, but I can't. It's no use.

I try to remember where I lived. I had to get the bus there, but it wasn't far. What was the name of the street? I think back to the car he drove that night. I feel the tightness of the red coat, the weight of my bag on my lap. The dark street leading away from the bus stop: did we turn left or right? I can't remember. Then the burning taste of the alcohol on my tongue, the lights which wavered and began to blur through the windscreen.

Then I remember the photograph. I find it, and spread it out onto my knee. I know we were in the garden: I remember the tree and the shadow it threw over the back of the house. It was the biggest one on our street, towering above the others. I remember the coolness underneath it; the feel of rough bark underneath my hands, and along my back. The splinters of dark wood that would be left behind. I would lie on the lower branches for hours, looking up at the sunlight pressing down on the leaves higher up, making the edges glow.

Now I am running, up the patchy stretch of green and towards the back of the house. Dark red brick, with white shutters, and a tiled grey roof, covered with moss. My bedroom was on the second floor. I painted the walls with my dad, I remember listening to him hum under his breath as he worked. Turquoise paint. The tinny radio playing Motown. 'River Deep, Mountain High'. Then I am lifted off the ground, holding my roller aloft, and he swings me round, pinching under my armpits. I scream for him to put me down, but I am laughing.

I see the front of the house now, the ivy that covered one side of the building. Ours was the only brick house on the street, and that made it special. All the others were wooden. *If there's a fire,* I hear my dad say, *our house will be the only survivor.*

Then the word comes to me, and before I have the chance to forget it, I write it on the piece of paper.

Hansgata.

That is the name of the street, I'm almost sure of it.

Without waiting any longer, I pull my coat back on and slip into the corridor. I can hear the sound of a television coming from behind a closed door, and I walk slowly past. Picking up Kylan's keys from the hall table, I open the front door.

23

It doesn't take me long to find a taxi.

I say the name of the street, terrified that the driver will wrinkle his brow: that he will tell me such a place doesn't exist. But he simply pulls away from the pavement.

As we move through the streets, I stare out of the window, looking for things I recognize. For a long time, there is nothing: it is too dark to see much. Then we pass a newsagent on the corner, and I can smell the damp rubber of the mat, see the lines of cigarette packets behind the counter.

We drive down a street lined with skinny, leafless trees, and a strange sensation passes through me, as if I am falling from a great height. This is it, I think, I recognize it. This is the street.

'What number?' the taxi driver says.

'Fourteen,' I answer, surprising myself.

I climb out and look up at the building. It's smaller

than I remember, but it is the same house. There are lights on in most of the windows, and I can see the flickering of a television screen behind the curtain in the front room. There is a path which runs through a small front garden, and I feel my mother grasp hold of my hand and pull me along it, towards the blue front door. I hear her complaining. *Come on, Elise.* I see my small hand, wrapped in her bigger one.

I stand in a tiled porch with a low seat on either side. I reach up to ring the doorbell, and see a hand with long red-painted fingernails. As I press it, the hand is mine again, the fingernails bitten to the quick.

I hear the familiar bell ring out, and panic. There are noises beyond and I begin to wonder what I will do if my mother or father opens the door. Quickly, I try to work out how old my father would be now. Seventy-seven, I think, as the hinges begin to creak.

Standing on the doorstep is a woman in her early thirties with dark brown hair and small neat pearl earrings.

'Can I help you?' she asks.

'I'm looking for someone who used to live here, some time ago,' I say.

'Well, we've been here for six years,' she says.

'There was a man and a woman living here,' I say,

wishing I could remember their names. I grasp after anything else I know. 'It was over twenty years ago.'

'I don't think I can help you,' she says. She moves to close the door.

'They're my parents,' I cry out, and the door stops moving. 'I've lost touch with them, and I need to find them.'

She looks round the edge of the door at me. 'Do you want to come in?' she asks.

She turns around, and I follow her into the house, shutting the door behind me. The hallway is dim, the walls green, cluttered with kids' shoes and school bags. As I walk through, I hear a girl's laughter echo down the wide wooden staircase.

'How many children do you have?' I ask.

'Three boys,' she says, without turning around.

'I have a son too,' I say. 'But he's grown up now.'

I stop in the doorway of the kitchen. There's a woman standing by the sink with her back to us, her long dark blonde hair falling over her shoulders. I watch her hands as she takes a plate from the water, washes it, and puts it on the draining board. She is looking out of the window, at the garden. As she begins to turn her head towards me, she is gone.

When I look up, the woman is watching me.

'I grew up here,' I say.

'It's a great house.'

'Do you know anything about the people who lived here before you?'

'Not much. They were an older couple, though. We did the sale through an agent so we didn't find out much about them.'

'Did you ever meet them?'

'No,' she says.

'And you wouldn't know where they moved on to?'

'I'm afraid not,' she says. 'I'm sorry I can't be more helpful. But you're welcome to look around the house if you want to.'

'I should probably be getting back,' I say. 'I'm staying with my son and I don't want him to worry.' The woman looks relieved. 'Do you think I could maybe come back another day and have a look? I have a lot of memories in this house, and as I mentioned, I lost touch with my parents. It would mean a lot to me.'

'If I'm here, I'm happy to let you look around,' she says.

I follow her out of the kitchen and back through the hallway.

'Thank you,' I say, when we reach the doorway. 'And thanks for answering my questions.'

'I'm sorry I couldn't be more helpful,' she says. 'I'm Lucy, by the way.' She holds her hand out to me.

'Elise,' I say, taking it in mine.

*

In the taxi on the way back to Kylan's, I try to think what I can do next. Maybe I can find the newspaper article my picture is from: it will be about a missing girl and not a car crash. I will take Kylan back to the valley, and we will look under the house. Then he will have to believe me.

I turn the key in the lock and walk into the hallway, dropping the key on the table.

A figure appears further down the corridor. I move closer and see it is Katya.

'It's all right, Kylan,' she calls, 'she's here.'

I turn the corner into the kitchen and see Kylan on the phone.

'She's just walked in,' he says into the receiver. 'She looks fine.' A pause. 'I'll let you know. Thanks, Dad.'

Kylan puts the phone back onto the hook.

'We've been so worried, Mum,' Kylan says. 'Where have you been?'

'I just popped out for a walk,' I say. 'I couldn't sleep.'

'Why didn't you let me know?' he says. 'I came in to check on you, and you were gone.'

'I didn't want to disturb you,' I say.

'I was about to phone the police,' Kylan says.

'Kylan,' I say, 'I'm a grown woman. Don't you think I can take care of myself?'

Kylan doesn't say anything.

'I'm glad you're back safely,' he says. 'We'd better go to bed. It's getting late, and we have work in the morning.'

He turns and walks away, leaving me standing in the corridor, wanting to explain again.

24

When I wake up, he is sitting on the edge of my bed. Outside the blue edges of the window, I can hear the constant underbelly rumblings of the city. I tell myself that he isn't really here, that he is just a memory. I kick him with my foot, trying to get him to disappear.

'What have you done to your hair?' he says.

I sit up, pulling my knees up close to my chest. It is really him. I scream.

'Marta,' he says, 'calm down. It's only me.'

I keep crying out, moving round to the other side of the bed. 'Get away from me,' I gasp.

Kylan comes into the room then, still wearing his pyjamas, his hair messy. 'What's going on?' he says.

I'm trembling now, staring at Hector, standing by the bed.

'Mum,' Kylan says. 'What's the matter?'

'I need him to get out of here,' I say. 'Please, Kylan. Make him leave.'

'He's driven through the night to get here. He was worried about you.'

I laugh. 'He's not worried,' I say. 'He's frightened. He thinks I'll tell you what he's done.'

Hector is staring at me.

'Mum, Dad has already told me,' Kylan says. 'He told me everything.'

I look from one to the other.

'You know?'

'Yes.' He sits down. 'I think you're over-reacting a little bit.'

My mouth drops open.

'It was a misunderstanding,' Kylan says. 'I can't believe you think Dad would do that. She's young enough to be his daughter.' He puts his hand on his father's shoulder. 'Dad needs our support right now. They can't fire him without evidence. If they try, we're going to fight it.'

'You don't understand,' I say. 'I'm not talking about the student. We need to go to the police.'

'Mum, you're not making any sense. Do you seriously not believe him?'

Hector is still watching me, not blinking. I recognize the slight smile at the corner of his mouth.

'Kylan, please,' I say. 'I need you to listen.'

Kylan stares at me.

Still Hector doesn't say anything. He just sits on the end of the bed and watches me.

'You don't understand,' I say. 'He took me.' Kylan looks at me blankly, and I start to cry with frustration.

Hector stands up. 'Marta,' he says.

'You know that's not my name,' I say. Kylan and Hector exchange glances.

'We think you should see somebody.' Hector crosses his arms. 'It's not easy to have to say this, but you haven't been well for a long time. I understand you've been under a lot of stress, with Kylan leaving home and me losing my job: things have been hard. But you're not making sense any more and we don't know how to help you.'

'You know I'm making sense,' I say. 'Tell him what you did.'

Kylan puts his hands on my shoulders, leaning down so he can look me in the eye.

'Mum,' he says, 'I know what Dad did. You need to calm down.'

'You don't know, Kylan,' I say. 'You won't let me explain.'

There is a horrible silence. 'I'm sorry, Mum,' Kylan says eventually. 'But I'm worried about you, we both are. You've stopped taking your pills—'

'I don't need my pills.'

'Just look at yourself, Marta,' Hector says. 'I don't know how you can say you are better without your medication.'

I reach for Kylan's hand. 'Please let me explain,' I say. Kylan waits. 'He took me from outside the ballet studio,' I say. 'He told me my family was dead. Look under the front porch, under the house. You have to believe me.'

Kylan stares at me.

'Please, Kylan,' I say. 'I'll show you. Let's go back to the house now, and I'll show you.'

He looks at Hector, then back at me.

'All right,' he says. 'We'll all go back to the house and have a look. Let's get dressed, I'll go and ring work and tell them I won't be coming in today.'

I can feel Hector staring at him, and I want to smile.

'Then we can go to the police?' I ask.

'Yes,' he says. 'We'll go to the police.'

*

We drive through grey streets, the early morning light making everything colourless. A big yellow cloud spreads across the sky behind the buildings, and the tension in my temples means a storm is coming.

In the reflection of the window, I see myself, my new

haircut which is really my old one. I brush the fringe out of my eyes and I am her again, on my way to ballet class, on my way home from school.

We drive past the edge of the park, the Palace hidden through the foliage. The trees along the avenue are bare black skeletons, and even the leaves at their feet are turned to dust now, carpeting the paths with fragments of old beauty.

I look round at Kylan in the back of the car.

'He's not going anywhere, you know,' Hector says, and I swing back round to look at him in the driver's seat. He glances at me. 'There's no need to keep checking on him.'

I turn to look out of the window as we pull into a parking space.

'Why are we stopping here?' I say.

'This is where I work,' Kylan says. 'I just need to pop in and get a few things.'

'I won't stay here with him,' I say.

'Come in, then,' Kylan says. 'You can meet everyone.'

We get out of the car and I follow him along the street. As we walk, I catch sight of us in the floor-length windows, Kylan looming tall, his sandy hair glinting in the sunlight. I feel his hand getting bigger around mine. I look down and see my flowered dress, my chubby legs and the small, black-patent Mary Jane shoes on my feet.

In the reflection, I see the white blonde hair, the big eyes and small round face. I am walking with my daddy. We are on our way to buy milk for breakfast. He hums under his breath, his hand warm in mine. From down here, I can only see the bottom of his face, his firm jaw line and Adam's apple. I squeeze his hand, wanting him to look down at me. But when he does, it is Kylan again.

We are walking up some wide stone steps now towards big brown double doors.

When we get into the lobby, he goes to speak to the receptionist. She has long dark hair and too much make-up on. They look over, then come towards me.

'Mrs Bjornstad,' she says, 'if you'd like to come with me?'

'I'll stay with my son,' I say.

The receptionist looks at Kylan. 'It'll only be for a few minutes, Mum,' he says. 'There's a man who wants to talk to you.'

'Who?' I ask. 'Someone you work with?'

'No,' he says slowly. 'A psychiatrist.'

I stare at him. 'Why is there a psychiatrist working in the bank?' I say.

Kylan puts his hand on my arm. 'Mum, I don't work here,' he says. 'This is a psychiatric facility and there is a man here who I think you should speak to.'

'But you told me we were going to the house,' I say. 'Why would you lie to me?' I feel the tears come.

'Mum, please don't cry. I really think this is for the best. We're worried about you. Please, will you speak to this man? I promise it won't take long.'

As I look at him, I see him as a little boy again, home from football practice, catching me staring out of the kitchen window. I see the same crease between his eyes, deeper now.

'Please, Mum,' he says. 'Do it for me. I'll wait right here for you.'

There are tears in his eyes. I don't want him to be upset. It will only take a second. 'OK,' I say, and let the girl lead me away. 'But stay here,' I say. 'Don't go.'

The girl leads me down a long dark corridor. She's holding a brown folder, a few sheets of white paper emerging from the top. The first few lines are visible.

Patient Name: *Marta Bjornstad.*

I stop and close my eyes. I can see that name, written until it covers a sheet of white lined paper. Over and over and over. Big scrawled letters, like a child's writing. Page after page. *Write it again.* I remember the way my hand shook, the words hardly coming out at all. The quivering nib, how difficult it was to clench my fingers around the pen. *Marta Bjornstad.* I see him put it back between my fingers again and again. *That is your name. Write it again. Write it again.*

'Mrs Bjornstad? Are you all right?'

I open my eyes and the girl is standing in the dim corridor, her big brown eyes glistening in the semi-darkness. I step forwards. We come to a polished wooden door with a brass plaque marked 'Room 4 – Dr Brun'. She knocks, and a man's voice answers.

'Come in.'

She pushes the door open. 'Your nine o'clock,' she says.

There are bookcases lining the far wall, a large mahogany desk, a comfortable-looking brown sofa with a red damask throw over the back, and a leather easy chair. On a rug in front of the sofa is a low table with a shelf underneath covered with magazines, neatly stacked.

A man with sloping shoulders and short legs is standing behind the desk. He has the beginnings of a greying beard, and small dark eyes.

The girl turns to leave but I'm standing in her way. 'Do come in, Mrs Bjornstad.' I stay where I am. He has a deep rumbling voice. 'There's nothing to be afraid of.'

I take a step into the room, and the girl squeezes past me and out into the corridor, pulling the door shut behind her. I put my hand out, onto the handle.

'Would you rather leave it open?' he says.

'Yes,' I say.

'Come and sit down,' he says, gesturing to the sofa.

I sit down, keeping my handbag over my arm. He takes a seat in the armchair and puts his hands on his knees.

'So what brings you in to see me today, Mrs Bjornstad?' he says.

'My son wanted me to come.'

He looks at me. I thought he would have a notepad to write things down.

'Why did he want you to come?'

'Because he thinks I'm losing my mind,' I say. I imagine Kylan's concerned face: it makes me want to go out and try to explain again.

'Why does he think that?' the man asks.

'He caught me smoking,' I say. 'And there was an incident yesterday.'

He raises his eyebrows. 'An incident?'

'He thinks I tried to steal a little girl.'

He doesn't look surprised. He waits.

'I thought she was somebody else,' I say. 'I thought she was in danger.'

'So you tried to rescue her?'

'Yes, but her father thought I was trying to steal her.' I laugh. 'I suppose it might have looked like that.'

There is a pause while he watches me without saying anything.

'And the smoking?' he asks eventually. 'You don't normally smoke?' he says.

'I used to.'

'And you've started again recently?'

'Yes,' I say.

'Why is that, do you think?'

'I don't know,' I say. 'I suppose I was bored.'

'Bored of what?'

'I don't know. Everything. I have a lot of time now Kylan has left me.'

'Your son?'

'Yes,' I say.

'When did he leave home?' he asks.

'A few months ago.'

'And you've been finding things hard since then?'

'Yes, but not because of that.'

'Why?'

'Because of my husband.'

He rubs his chin. 'What has your husband done?' he says.

I stare at him, unable to answer.

'Mrs Bjornstad?' he says. 'What has your husband done to make things hard?'

He waits.

'Do you mind if I call you Marta?' he says.

'Yes,' I say.

He stares at me then, a question marking his features. 'You do mind?'

'It's not my name,' I say.

The doctor reaches out and slides my file off his desk. 'Marta Bjornstad?' he says. 'Is that not right?'

'No,' I say.

He looks at the file again. 'What is your name?' he asks.

'Elise Sandvik,' I say.

He lowers his eyes to the file again, turns over a page. 'And your address?'

'14 Hansgata.'

The doctor gets up and moves over to his desk. He presses a button.

'Yes?' I can hear the girl's voice, tinny and small, in the office.

'The file for my nine o'clock is for a Marta Bjornstad, and I have an Elise Sandvik here. Should she be in a different office?'

There is a short silence. 'That is Marta Bjornstad you have with you, Doctor.'

'She says her name is Elise Sandvik.'

Another silence. 'I have her son here, and he says her name is Marta Bjornstad.'

The doctor looks at me. He presses the button again. 'Thanks,' he says.

He sits down again. He doesn't say anything, just waits for me to explain. I look at him.

'You're not Marta Bjornstad?' he says eventually.

'My son thinks I am,' I say.

'But you're not?'

'No,' I say.

'Why does your son think you're Marta Bjornstad?'

'It's the name my husband gave me,' I say.

'Your husband calls you Marta?'

'He changed it.'

'Why?'

'Because he wanted me to forget who I was before.'

'Before you got married?'

'No,' I say. 'Before he took me.'

'He took you?'

I nod.

'What do you mean?'

I sigh. 'He took me from outside the ballet studio,' I say. 'He kept me under his house.'

'He kept you against your will?'

I nod. The man looks at me for a long time then.

'You realize that is a serious allegation?'

'I'm just telling you what happened.'

He picks up my file and reads for a moment.

'Your husband mentioned on the phone that you have been on medication for some time. Is that true?'

'He made me take it.'

'Your husband?'

'Yes,' I say.

'Do you know what the medication does?' he says.

'He said it would make me better.'

He looks at his notes again. 'Your husband said that you had been taking the medication since before he met you. That you started taking it because of the death of your parents.'

'That's not true,' I say. 'He's a liar. He gave it to me.'

The doctor watches me. 'The medication you are on has to be prescribed by a doctor,' he says. 'Your husband wouldn't be able to get hold of it unless he had a serious psychological condition.'

'We go to the doctor in the village,' I say. 'He's Hector's friend. He's had him fooled from the beginning.'

He taps his pen against his leg. He writes something, and then looks up at me.

'Your parents died when you were eighteen, is that correct?'

'He told me that, but it isn't true.' I pause. 'They might be still alive.'

The doctor looks in the file again.

'Have you ever tried to kill yourself, Mrs Bjornstad?'

I think of the cold water of the ocean, the blue blur of lights under the surface.

'No,' I say.

'You haven't?'

'I didn't go down there to kill myself.'

'Down where?'

'To the sea. We were on holiday.'

'You were on holiday and you wanted to kill yourself?'

'No,' I say. 'I wasn't trying to kill myself. I just didn't want to come back up.'

A tear drips onto my trouser leg, leaving a wet black circle. The doctor writes something else.

'Your husband mentioned that when you met, he pulled you out of the water, that he saved your life. He said that you had an eating disorder and that you were clinically depressed.'

'We didn't meet then,' I interrupt. 'That's just what he told people.'

'When did you meet, then?'

'He took me.'

The doctor waits for me to continue.

I sigh. I'm so tired. 'I was waiting outside the ballet studio and he took me. He drugged me and took me under the house.'

The doctor narrows his eyes. 'Why would he do that?'

'Because he wanted a wife.'

'So he took you?'

'Yes,' I say. 'He told me later that he had found me on the doorstep, and that he took care of me when I was ill, but he made me that way.'

'He deliberately made you ill?'

'He knew what he was doing. He didn't give me a lot of food: made me dependent on him. And when that wasn't working, he told me my parents were dead.'

'How old were you when this happened?'

'Eighteen,' I say.

'He kept you under the house for how long?'

'I don't know,' I say. 'About two years.'

'And then he let you out, and you married him?'

He doesn't believe me.

'He made me believe he saved my life,' I say. 'He gave me a new name. He was the only person I had left.'

'When did you start remembering these things, Mrs Bjornstad?'

'I stopped taking my pills, and I started seeing things.'

'You were hallucinating?'

'I thought I was, but they weren't hallucinations. They were things that happened.'

'What kind of things were you seeing?'

'A blonde girl.'

'How long has it been since you last took your medication?'

'I'm not sure,' I say. 'I stopped taking it a few weeks after my son left, so a couple of months?'

He starts writing again. 'How long did the hallucinations last?'

'They weren't hallucinations,' I say.

'OK,' he says, smiling tightly. 'How long did you see these things for?'

'I'm not sure. It varies.'

'And were they triggered by anything in your surroundings?'

I try to think back. 'I don't know,' I say. 'But the more they come back, the more I know they really happened. I remember them.'

'And they're still coming back now?'

I nod.

He writes something else in his notes and then he looks at his watch. 'Our time is up, unfortunately, Mrs Bjornstad,' he says, standing. 'If you could wait here for a second, I'll be right back.'

I stand up. He walks across the room, and through the door, pulling it shut behind him.

He has left my file on the table. I walk across the room and open it. His writing is slanty, hard to read, but I make out some of what he has written.

Experienced serious depressive symptoms and attempted suicide after traumatic event (parents' death) at age 18, prescribed medication (check previous medical notes for diagnosis?). Since ceasing to take medication, frequent and increasing hallucinations. Believes these to be a re-living of true events. Developed to paranoid delusions that husband is threat to her wellbeing. Believes husband, Hector Bjornstad, abducted her, and that previously she was Elise Sandvik. Perhaps early misdiagnosis of depression – depressive and psychotic symptoms could suggest schizoaffective disorder?

I read on to the end of the page. Under the section marked THREAT TO HERSELF OR OTHERS? he has written: *Yes, keep in for observation.*

I walk out of the room and down the corridor. The doctor is standing in the reception area speaking to Hector and Kylan in a low voice. Kylan's eyes are red. Hector's face is blank but I can see a small smile at the corner of his mouth.

I step forward. 'I won't stay here,' I say.

The doctor turns around. 'Mrs Bjornstad,' he says. 'I said I would come back in a moment.'

'I know what you're planning on doing, and I won't stay here. I want to stay with my son.'

'Mum, please,' Kylan says, a tear rolling down his cheek. 'Just do what the doctor asks.'

'You promised me we'd go to the house,' I say. 'I need to show you so you will believe me. I need to go to the police.'

Kylan puts his warm hands over my cold ones. 'Mum,' he says. 'You need to stop this. It's really upsetting.'

'Please, Kylan,' I say. 'I know you don't want to believe it, but go to the house and look under the front step. Promise me.'

Kylan doesn't take his eyes off me. He nods.

Hector steps forward. 'Can you give us a moment?' he says to the doctor.

The doctor begins to move away, back towards his office. 'I'll come back.'

We stand together, Kylan, Hector and I, close to the door, within a few metres of the reception desk. The girl concentrates on typing at her computer.

Hector takes a step towards me. I feel myself begin to shake.

'Get away from me,' I say.

'I'm sorry this has to happen, Marta,' he says. 'But really you have left us no choice. I don't feel I can give you the care you need any more.'

I stare at him. 'My name is Elise!' I shout.

'I've only ever wanted to make you happy.'

My palms are sweating and my chest is tight.

'I don't know what you thought was under the house,' he says. 'But I assure you there isn't anything there now.' He looks straight at me then.

I launch myself at him, kicking and hitting him. He doesn't fight back: he stands there and lets me pummel him, my blows rebounding from his soft jumpered chest.

'Tell them the truth,' I scream.

'There is nothing to tell,' he says.

People appear out of nowhere, pulling me backwards, and the doctor is there again. Someone holds on to my arms and a needle appears. The last thing I see before everything goes black is Kylan's little-boy face, his eyes wide, the tears running down his cheeks. I want to reach my hands out to him, to tell him I will make it all better. But everything starts to slip away.

25

I wake up in a small square room. I am lying in a low bed with a narrow metal frame, tucked in tight, under the clean white covers.

There is an electric strip light running across the ceiling which is not turned on.

The room is in semi-darkness, and when I sit up, I think I see the shadow of a man sitting on the end of my bed, waiting for me to wake up. I kick out with my legs, and the man disappears.

My eyes adjust to the darkness. There's a door with a small glass window: shatterproof, which throws a warm yellow square of light on the linoleum floor. The walls are white and smooth, and in the corner of the room is a sink. There is a box with the fingers of gloves protruding from it, and a large canister of hand sanitizer. There's no mirror above the sink. A toilet to my right, plumbed into the wall.

I get out of bed. I am wearing a hospital gown, tight

across the chest and open at the back. I turn the door handle, but it's locked.

I start to shout then. *Help me, please. Open the door. Anybody. Please.*

I bang on the glass until it rattles. I look around for something I can use to break it, but everything in the room is secured to the ground.

A woman's face appears at the door. She has red hair in a neat bun, and a warm, round face. She puts her finger to her lips.

I step back from the door and she unlocks it.

'Is everything all right?' she asks.

'I can't stay here,' I say.

'It's only for the night,' she says.

'I want to see my son,' I say.

'Your son is at home,' she says. 'He's coming for you in the morning. It's best you try and get some rest now.'

'I don't want to stay here,' I say. 'Not on my own.'

'It's only for one night, Mrs Bjornstad,' she says. 'They're making plans to move you tomorrow.'

'There's nothing wrong with me,' I say. 'I can stay with my son.'

'The doctor wanted to keep you in,' she says. 'Just for tonight.' Her face softens. 'Do you want anything to eat?

I think the kitchen is closed but I can try and get you something?'

'Can I call my son?' I ask.

'I can't let you use the phone,' she says. 'But he's coming in the morning.'

'Alone?' I ask.

'I'm afraid I don't know.'

'Can we put the lights on?' I ask.

'Sure,' she says. 'If you need anything else, just press the button on the wall.'

'I'm sorry for the noise,' I say. 'I just wasn't sure where I was.'

'That's all right,' she says. 'I hope you get some sleep.'

As she leaves, I hear the click of the lock behind her.

26

All night, I pace from one end of the room to the other.

I was out there, driving through the vast valleys, and I came to the city, only to end up here.

I tell myself not to be, but I am angry with Kylan for not believing me. I came to him because I needed help.

There's no clock in the room, so it is hard to tell what time it is. The only window is the one in the door which leads to the corridor. For some reason, they have removed the watch from my wrist.

Outside in the corridor, the other lights start to go on, and I know it must be nearly morning.

When breakfast arrives, two powdery eggs and toast, I try to ask the new nurse.

'Is my son coming?' I ask.

She barely looks at me, putting the tray on the cabinet by the bed.

'Excuse me,' I say, 'can you please tell me if I am leaving here today?'

'Someone will be here to see you shortly,' she says. 'I just deliver the breakfasts.'

'What time is it?' I ask.

'Nine o'clock,' she says, as she shuts and locks the door behind her.

I sit on the edge of the bed, waiting.

*

A young doctor with a clipboard comes into the room.

'Morning, Mrs Bjornstad,' he says, reading the name from his chart. 'How are you feeling?'

'What time is it?' I ask.

'Just gone eleven,' he says. 'You haven't eaten your breakfast.'

'I'm not hungry,' I say. 'When is my son coming?'

'Visiting hours are between four and nine p.m.'

'I thought I was being moved today.'

The doctor smiles at me as if I am a child. 'It's not as simple as that, I'm afraid, Mrs Bjornstad. You won't be moved until you are referred elsewhere,' he says. 'We need to determine your diagnosis.'

'How do you do that?'

'A mixture of group and one-on-one therapy sessions. You'll have one group session every morning, and one evaluation every afternoon.'

'And the rest of the time?'

'Free time, for contemplation in your room.'

My chest tightens. 'How long will I be here for?'

'Until we can decide what is wrong with you, and then you will be sent to a different facility for treatment.'

'But, Doctor,' I say, sitting up straighter and pulling my gown around me, 'there is nothing wrong with me.'

The doctor smiles again. 'That is what we are here to determine.'

'No,' I say. 'There's been a mistake. I need to speak to the police.'

'For now,' he says, 'we just need to focus on making you feel better.'

'But you need to investigate,' I say. 'I am the victim of a crime.'

'Everything you say will be kept on file, Mrs Bjorn-stad.' He sounds bored.

I grab his hand. 'I need to speak to someone,' I say. 'My name is Elise Sandvik. We need to find proof that I am a missing person.'

'I don't think that should be the priority at the moment,' the doctor says, shaking himself free of me and rising to his feet. 'We need to focus on your recovery.' He picks a small white cup of pills from the breakfast tray and hands it to me. 'Starting with your medication.'

I take the cup, nodding my head.

'Please can I have my watch back?' I ask.

'We can't let you have anything with glass in it, I'm afraid,' he says.

'Can I have a clock, then?' I ask. 'I need to know the time.'

He half smiles, writing something on my chart. 'I'll mention it to the nurse,' he says.

When he is gone, I tip the pills into the sink.

The hot anger rises. Why won't they listen to me? Even though it happened over twenty years ago, there must be files on my disappearance. It shouldn't be hard to trace.

I feel like throwing things against the wall, like shouting and screaming, but I know that will only prove them right.

*

Shortly after I have eaten dinner, Kylan comes to see me. Despite me asking, they still haven't given me a clock, so I can't say what time it is. Though he smiles when he enters the room, his eyes are a little bloodshot and he looks exhausted.

'Hello, Mum,' he says, sitting next to me.

'Hi,' I say.

He looks around the room. 'How are you feeling?'

'How do you think I'm feeling?' I say. I don't want to be, but I am annoyed with him. I have spent the whole day in this room, and I am sick of it.

'Look, Mum,' he says, 'I'm so sorry about what happened yesterday. I couldn't sleep at all last night.'

'Neither could I,' I say.

He looks at the narrow bed, the sink, the locked door. 'I don't like thinking about you in here.'

'Take me home with you, then,' I say.

'I can't,' he says. 'The doctors say it's the best place for you.'

I can't believe he is going to leave me in here.

'There's something I need to tell you,' he says. 'When I couldn't sleep last night, I looked up the name you mentioned on the Internet, to see if I could find anything out.'

'Oh, Kylan,' I say. 'What did you find? If we can prove it, I can get out of here . . .'

He puts his hand over mine. 'I couldn't find anything, Mum,' he says.

I feel my mouth fall open. 'Where did you look?'

'I searched the Internet for the name, and nothing relevant came up.'

'Did you call the police?' I say. 'The police must have records of it.'

'No,' Kylan says. 'If it were true, there would be something on the Internet about it.'

'Maybe you were looking in the wrong places,' I say. 'We need to ask the police.'

'Mum,' Kylan says, his voice raw, 'you need to stop this now. I looked, and I couldn't find anything. I think you need to accept it.'

I stare at him: his red eyes, and messy hair, and grey skin. I have done this to him, I think. But I know he would have found something if he looked hard enough, if he spelt the name correctly.

Then I think that maybe he doesn't want to, maybe he didn't even look. If he did, he would have to admit that his father did those terrible things. Hector, who, despite everything, has been a good father. He would have to report him, or help me to. And then Hector would go to jail, and Kylan would be visiting him instead of me, locked in a room worse than this.

If I push this, I will ruin Kylan's life, and I don't want to do that. I would rather stay here for ever than make him unhappy.

I swallow, and nod my head.

Kylan squeezes my hand. 'I know it can't be easy,' he says, 'and we're going to get you all the help you need. It would just be a lot easier if you stop fighting us on it.'

He pauses. 'I'll speak to the doctor and see if we can't get you moved from here.'

He gets up then.

'Will you come back soon?' I ask him as he reaches the door.

'I'll be back at the weekend. Look after yourself, Mum.'

'Kylan,' I say when he is at the door, 'can you ask them again if I can have a clock? They've taken my watch away.'

He looks so sad. I feel something shift in my chest.

When he is gone, the tears rise up in my eyes. And I know then what I need to do.

27

The light flashes brightly into the room, and I open my eyes. Laura is at the window, pulling back the thick blue curtains so I can see the garden. She turns and smiles at me.

'Today's the day,' she says.

I sit up in the big comfortable bed with its blue sheets and solid white headboard. There is a picture of Kylan and me on the bedside table, beside a lamp with an ugly flowered lampshade.

All the rooms are like this: homely, so it seems like we are safe.

There's a large alarm clock which glows all through the night. I'm not allowed to set the alarm for fear of disturbing the other residents. It reads 9:00: the time they always wake us.

Laura comes over with a tray and rests it on my knees. I'm glad I don't have to iron her crisp white uniform.

Cereal with milk: something I chose myself. They tell

us we have lots of choices. Toast, cereal, eggs at the weekends. I had never had breakfast in bed before I came here, and now I have it every day.

There are two bowls on the tray, and Laura slides one off onto her own knee.

'You're eating with me?' I ask.

'I told you we would do everything together today.'

We eat in silence, and when we are finished, Laura clears our bowls away.

'I'll leave you to get ready,' she says. 'We need to be out by eleven.'

'I'll meet you in the lobby,' I say.

I get out of bed and go over to the window. Outside, the lawn stretches over a little hill and towards the lake. There are trees around the edges, weeping willows, their branches trembling along the surface of the water. Everything is bright and green; the sun is shining. It is spring now.

In the bathroom, my navy suit is hanging on the back of the door. After my shower, I dry myself and pull it on. I sit at the dressing table, covered with the framed pictures of Kylan. They asked me if I wanted anything brought here from the old house, and I made a list. These photographs from the hallway, my remaining clothes, and my book: *How To Be a Good Wife*. These are the only things in the room that are really mine. Sometimes, I imagine that this is my room, but it isn't really. I know it could be taken away if the fees stop being paid. I don't have any of my own money to keep paying them, and sometimes I wonder how long it will last.

I take out the hairdryer. The warmth is pleasant, and I shut my eyes. When I open them, I see my mother behind me in the mirror. Gently, she pulls my hair back and dries it. Her fingers are deft and gentle on my scalp, reminding me of long car journeys as a child when she would play with my hair until I fell asleep.

This is what it's like now. They come and they go, without warning. I hold on to them while they are here but it becomes harder and harder to let them go.

And there are the bad moments too, the black flashes that come so forcefully and vividly, it is as if I am there again. I don't see the girl any more: it is me that is trapped in that room, with my aching body and empty stomach. Sometimes, I wake up screaming: I hate to make the nurses come running. The flashes mostly come at night, or from something unexpected: the smell of a cleaning product, or the creaking of a bed spring. I am learning what to avoid. Hector is always there: even when I cannot see him.

At 10:55, before I leave the room, I pick up the present

from the table by the door. I wrapped it myself, in the paper they gave me when I asked. It is brown and plain, not what I would have chosen, but it is better than nothing.

In the lobby, Laura is waiting for me. She has changed out of her uniform into a pretty pink dress. I have never seen her dark hair down before: out of her regulation bun, it reaches her shoulders.

'You look lovely, Elise,' she says.

I smile. 'So do you.'

'Well,' she says. 'Are you ready?'

I walk towards the open front door, into the square of sunlight.

*

There is a black car waiting for us. It's different to the vehicle I arrived here in, and I wonder if it is one of the staff's, or if they hired it specially. Everything has been carefully planned for today so that it runs smoothly. It is rare, they told me, for us to be allowed out, but they can make exceptions, on special occasions.

We drive out along the gravel path, through an avenue of tall green trees, their silver bark catching the light. When I arrived, it was hard to see out of the small windows of the van. I remember the heavy fear, my hands gripping the shiny faux-leather seat, but when I stepped out and saw the building, I was surprised. It was an old stone house, with faded blue paintwork and white shutters. There were lots of big, wide windows, and a grand stone porch, surrounded by decorative columns. It looked out over a small lake, with open fields beyond.

I had imagined somewhere small with artificial light, like the room I had been put in at the facility. I suppose I am lucky, that I am being taken care of.

The drive is long. I look out of the window at the sunlight dappling the fields. When I feel nervous, I look over at Laura, and feel better. I have told her about Hector. I'm not sure whether she believed me or not, but she kept her face so flat and calm, nodding in all the right places so that it didn't seem to matter. She and the other doctors listen to me when I talk. They call me by my real name. In the beginning, they tried to show me how to control the memories, how to stop them, but I made it clear that I wanted to remember. It is all I live for now. I take the good with the bad.

There is a light airy library in the house where I like to sit. The room has huge windows overlooking the lake, and patio doors that they open in the mornings now that it is warmer, so that we can go outside when we feel like it. It's nice, to watch the ducks gliding on the surface, to feel the sun on my face, but there are limits, just as in there were in the valley. I must not leave the grounds, or go into the woodland beyond the lake.

I sit by the window and remember. There is nothing to do now, nothing to distract me, but I am glad: I want the memories now. Sometimes they are the same as ones I have had before, and sometimes they are new, or slightly different. Each time, they are so vibrant and bright that I don't want to come back from the past. I want to stay there, with those people, but I know that isn't possible.

I haven't made many friends, but I suppose I am out of practice. Sometimes I smile at the other residents, and they smile back. I suppose I have Laura, though I know it is her job to be nice to me.

Kylan comes to see me once a week. After our conversation in the facility, I don't try to explain any more, about what happened. I tell him what I have had for breakfast, about craft classes and group-therapy sessions: my daily routine. I listen to him talk about the wedding, the house they are thinking of buying. He never mentions his father, unless I ask him. Sometimes, when he goes home, my face aches from smiling.

I watch the fields and forests fly past the window. I

must have slept for a while, because soon, Laura is tapping me on my shoulder, and telling me we are here.

*

By the church clock, it is 12:25 when we arrive. As I pull myself out of the car, I am startled by the number of people in the churchyard. They seem crammed onto the flagstones, a mass of writhing colour. I feel the faces turn to look at me, and I long to slip back into the car and let it drive me away. Then I feel Laura's hand on my arm: the car door shutting behind me.

I see Kylan, standing on the pavement before the church gates, looking for someone. Just as I am wondering who, he turns and sees me and starts walking towards us.

'You're here,' he says, pulling me into a hug.

'We just arrived,' I say.

'You look lovely, Mum,' he says.

I smile. 'So do you,' I say, looking at his stiff morning suit.

'I'm a bit uncomfortable,' he says. 'I didn't think it would be this warm in April.'

The old crease deepens between his eyes, and I realize he is nervous. 'It's going to be wonderful,' I say.

He squeezes my arm. 'I hope so,' he says. 'I'll show you to your seat.'

He leads me through the churchyard towards the door, and people move apart to let us through. I look for the familiar thinning brown hair, the walking stick, but he is nowhere to be seen.

As Kylan leads me through the entrance of the church, my eyes adjust to the dimness, and for a moment, I can't make out anything inside. I feel myself grip his arm.

'Don't worry, Mum,' Kylan says. 'Dad isn't here yet.'

I breathe out. Laura is right behind me. I wonder if they planned for Hector to arrive later: how much additional stress this must have caused. I see how hard it will be for Kylan, to juggle us for the rest of his life. I want to tell him that he doesn't need to worry: I am determined to stay calm, not to ruin the day.

Kylan leads me to the front of the church, to a sign marked 'Reserved' in the front pew.

'Best seats in the house,' Laura says, and Kylan smiles at her.

'You should be able to see everything from here,' he says.

'Thanks, Kylan,' I say. 'This is perfect.'

'Dad will be on the other side,' he says. 'I hope that's all right.'

'We'll be great here, won't we, Elise?' Laura says.

Kylan balks at the name, and Laura blushes.

'I'm fine, Kylan,' I say. 'Honestly. Go and enjoy your day. And stop worrying about me.'

Kylan looks at me, and I pull him into a hug. 'You look so good,' I whisper.

As I let him go, I see him smile, and for a moment, he is a little boy again, nervous about running the hundred-metres race at the school sports day. He walks down the aisle and back towards the entrance of the church, stopping to talk to some people along the way. I see him shake hands with an old school friend, laughing at something the man says, and I realize how proud I am of him.

'He's a lovely man,' Laura says.

'Yes,' I say.

'You've done a good job with him,' she says, and I smile.

＊

It is warm in the church: people fan themselves with their orders of service, and there's a buzz of chatter in the air. I keep an eye out: every time I turn around, I am momentarily disorientated by the menagerie of bright hats and dresses.

When the church is almost full, I turn my head and see Hector and his mother walking down the aisle, arm in arm. Hector is without his stick, but he is still a little stooped, and I am struck by how small he looks. Kylan told me that Matilda has moved back into the house with him, to take her old job back, I suppose. She must be happy about that. I take hold of Laura's hand.

'Is that him?' she whispers, and I nod.

A few minutes pass before I risk another glance at him. He is sitting across the wide aisle, boxed into the pew by his mother and a group of people I don't know. As I turn my head, I see that he is staring at me, a still, flat look on his face that makes me tremble. He doesn't look angry, or sad. There is a blankness that I find more disconcerting.

Hector looks away, towards the front of the church, and as I follow his gaze I see that Kylan is entering from the side chapel with his best man. They take their places at the altar rail, and Kylan shakes his friend's hand. He rocks backward on his heels, glancing behind him.

Just then, the organ starts up, and everyone turns to the back of the church. I see a white shadow in the doorway, lit up by the sunshine outside. Slowly, arm in arm with a sturdy grey-haired man, she walks forward. The wedding march begins. *Step left, step together, step right.* A gauzy veil covers her face, and for a moment, the man at her side falls away, and it is me again, walking down the aisle towards Hector. I want to reach out for her, to tell her to get out of the church and run as fast as she can, but as I look down at Laura's hand over mine, I know I am too late for that. It is Katya, underneath that veil, and even through the material, I can see she is smiling.

As she approaches, I turn to look at Kylan. As soon as I see his face, I feel the tears begin to push at the back of my throat. He is smiling, his eyes filled with joy, and excitement, and so many other things. That is what a husband should look like, I think. Katya kisses her father on the cheek, squeezes his arm, and takes two steps to her place beside Kylan at the altar.

*

When the ceremony is over, Laura makes sure we are one of the first to reach the doorway of the church. Hector waits in his seat. I am not sure if it has been planned this way, or if he can't get out quickly because of his knee.

My throat is still a little tight from the tears, but I feel lighter as I step out into the sunshine.

The courtyard is bright. Blinking, I see the bride and groom are standing to one side, waiting to greet people. Laura and I approach them.

They are laughing about something, and when they turn to us, they are smiling.

'That was perfect,' I say.

'I'm so glad you could come,' Katya says. The sunlight is behind her, making it hard to see her face clearly.

'I wouldn't have missed it,' I say. 'You look so lovely.'

'Thank you,' she says. 'You are looking very well yourself, Mrs—' She stops herself.

'You're Mrs Bjornstad now,' I say, and I laugh.

Kylan puts his arm around her. 'I suppose you are,' he says. 'Mr and Mrs Bjornstad.'

'I brought you a present, Katya,' I say, holding out the parcel under my arm.

Katya blushes. 'Thank you,' she says. She takes my hand and squeezes it, and for a moment, it is not Katya I see before me, but the girl I used to be, the light catching her long blonde hair. She smiles, a fearless, familiar smile, which makes my stomach ache.

Then it's Katya again. 'Shall I open it now?' she is saying.

'Save it,' I say.

'Thanks so much for coming, Mum,' Kylan says. 'I know it can't have been easy.'

I smile, pulling him into a hug, and this time, he doesn't move away first.

'We'll see you at the reception,' Katya says. 'It's only a short walk to the house from here.'

'We might take the car,' Laura says.

'You can go there now if you like,' Katya says. 'Everything's ready and my mum should be heading there soon.'

I let the people behind me greet the bride and groom.

'Are you ready to go now?' Laura asks me.

I nod, and we go to find the car.

'What was the present?' Laura asks as we slide in.

'A book,' I say. 'I was given it on my wedding day, and I thought I should pass it on.'

Laura turns back to the road ahead.

Making myself comfortable, I imagine Katya tearing off the wrapping paper and revealing the old tattered copy of *How To Be a Good Wife*. I can imagine her and Kylan laughing at the old-fashioned phrasing: belittling the demands that were so much a part of my married life. I don't need it any more.

*

Soon, the reception is in full swing. The house is as beautiful as Kylan said, a yellow wooden building that skirts the edge of the fjord, with a long sloped lawn leading down to the water. The day is perfect, and the people milling about are smiling, their cheeks flushed from sun and champagne.

Laura and I have been sitting in the shade, watching

the party. Laura has spread her legs out in the sun, and she is on her second glass of wine. It's hard not to be relaxed when the weather is so nice, especially after the long winter, and with everything going so well. Kylan has come over a few times to check up on us, but I actually prefer it when we are left alone. I ask Kylan where his father is, and he tells me he has taken Matilda home. I have been introduced to Katya's parents, who seemed a little nervous, unsure of what to say, as if they were meeting a celebrity. I just nodded and smiled, as I have done all day. It is all I seem to do these days, and I have become quite used to it.

I like sitting here, out of the way, where I can watch the festivities. I can imagine blonde-haired children running across this lawn, a pregnant Katya smiling in the sunshine, a cool glass of water in her hand. I am like a lion in the shade, apparently resting, but actually waiting for the right moment. I know it will come, and I have waited so long now that a little longer won't make any difference.

There is a jazz band out here, and soon, people start to dance on the grass. Though it is only 4:10, some people have removed their shoes and socks. Laura is tapping her foot to the music.

There is food laid out on a table in the shade: a buffet

to help yourself to. I'm not hungry, but Laura brings me back a plate anyway, and I pretend to eat. After we have finished, a young man comes over to ask Laura to dance. She blushes, looking at me. I nod, smile, and tell her it is fine. She sits for a moment, her eyes squinting in the sunlight, and I can tell she is weighing up whether she is allowed to dance: she is supposed to be working, after all. But eventually, she gets up, smiles at me, and lets the young man draw her away.

To start with, they dance near me, the man leaning close and Laura jumping away slightly. She looks over at me, and I can tell she is embarrassed. She knows she should keep an eye on me. But gradually, she lets the man lead her into the throng of the other dancers, and after some minutes her attention wanders.

I glance around the lawn but I can't see Kylan or Katya. Slowly, I get out of my seat and walk into the house. I am ready with my excuse, but it is deserted: cool and shady and dim. All the doors and windows are open, the shutters thrown back, and I walk through unnoticed. As I reach the front hall, I hear the clattering of dishes from what must be the kitchen. I unlatch the front door and walk out.

The drive is cluttered with empty cars; I weave my way through. Before I know it, I am out on the road, hidden from view by the heavy evergreen trees that mark the territory of the house, dappling the road with sunlight. I walk quickly in the direction of the church and the town.

The heat has dislodged a warm, earthy smell from the dark trees, and I can hear the distant music. Kicking off my high heels and looping them over my wrist, I break into a run, watching the forest rush by me out of the corner of my eye. There isn't a soul on the road, and it doesn't take long to reach the village.

There is a bus stop on the main stretch and I stand by it, slipping my shoes back on, trying to make myself presentable. I check the timetable, before remembering I have no way of knowing the time. Soon, my feet begin to ache and I sit down. It can't be long, I think, but without a watch, time stretches. At every moment, I think I will see Kylan or Laura running down the road from the house.

Finally, the bus approaches. I step onto it. The bus driver smiles at me. I ask him where the end of the line is, then I buy a ticket, counting out the change onto the counter. It's the last of the money from my old purse, and it isn't quite enough, but he waves me on anyway.

I find a seat at the back. When we start to move, I feel an excitement rise in my chest. We drive back the way

I have walked, and as we pass the house, I duck down in my seat. Soon, we are long gone, and I relax, looking out of the window. I wonder if they have noticed yet.

The bus is quiet for most of the journey. There is a young man with blond hair who reminds me a little of Kylan, but I don't speak to him. Kylan and Katya will be leaving for their honeymoon soon, standing at the very edge of their new lives together. For a moment, I feel a pull of sadness, but I tell myself again that I am doing what is best.

I slip my hand into my bag and smooth out the scrap of newspaper I have saved. The picture of my family underneath the tree in the garden. Whenever I look at the picture, which is often, I think how sad it is that I didn't realize at the time how lucky I was, just to be standing there, so close to them. All I cared about that day was the prickling sweat running down my back: I wanted to go inside where it was cool. Now all I have are impressions and longings.

When I catch my first glimpse of the sea, the sun has begun to lower towards the horizon. I lean forward in my seat, watching the light shift across the water; the waves crash against the cliffs.

I get off the bus at the last stop, and walk down towards the shore. I can smell the sea, and I am reminded again of the taste of rock candy, crunching between my teeth. Once I reach the sand, I kick off my shoes and walk out barefoot towards an outcrop of rocks overlooking the beach.

Settling myself, I look back the way I have come. The beach is long and flat, the sand coarse and dotted with small shells. There are grey cliffs behind me, dropping to the rocks where I am sitting, and more, further out to sea. The beach is completely empty, but through the brisk wind, I hear a girl laughing. I see a flash of blonde hair, down on the shore, and I get up from the rocks and run down to the beach. Following the sounds of laughter, I run and run until my lungs burn and I am right at the edge of the water, watching the waves lap the shore, alone. This is what it's like: with a certain turn of light, or a familiar sound, they are here with me, these people from the past. In the thrill of remembrance, I am her again. But just as quickly, the moment passes, and I am back in the present, with only the renewed pain of everything I have lost.

And then I think of the message, written inside the back cover of *How To Be a Good Wife*, waiting to be found. Perhaps it never will be, but they are words I needed to say. It makes me smile to think of Katya taking the book down from a shelf, in a quiet lull between moments of motherly chaos, and finding my handwriting. Perhaps she will tell Kylan that I did say goodbye after all, that I was happy for them. That having my son was the best thing that ever happened to me, and that because of him, I would not change anything. And I hope that, maybe, they will understand what I am about to do.

I look behind me once more, but the beach is deserted. I start to walk along the edge, towards the rocks. Clambering across them, I am taken back to our holiday on the island, when I walked out to the water, thinking at every moment I would fall. When I am far round enough, I take off my clothes, and fold them into a neat pile. I sit down, listening to the breaking of the waves. For a moment, I look down into the dark water, and then, I let myself go.

Acknowledgements

I would like to thank the following:

The whole team at Picador for making me feel immediately at home. My wonderful editor, Francesca Main, for her careful thoughts, and for motivating me to make this book the very best it can be. Jennifer Weis and Mollie Traver at St Martin's Press for their comments and insights.

All at Toby Eady Associates for teaching me about the industry, and then for taking me on. Jamie Coleman for his humour, patience and brilliance. Zaria Rich for her helpfulness and advice. Nicole for her warmth, efficiency and endless cups of green tea. Toby Eady for his astute wisdom. Samar Hamman for her directness, honesty and kindness. Jennifer Joel and Clay Ezell at ICM; Marco Vigevani and Jan Michael for their hard work on my behalf.

Dr Simone Hughes at Creative Focus and Dr Diana Lalor at Cottesloe Counselling Centre for their insights into the realities of post-traumatic shock syndrome. Many books and journal articles have been important in researching this book, but I would like to mention *Trauma and Recovery* by Dr Judith Hermann, especially her work on the effects of captivity.

Professor Andrew Motion and Susanna Jones for their encouragement on the Royal Holloway MA in Creative Writing. The two-syllable group: Kat Gordon, Tom Feltham, Carolina Gonzalez-Carvajal, Rebecca Lloyd James, Lucy Hounsom, Liz Gifford, and Liza Klaussmann. Ellie Guttridge in the press office for spreading the word.

The teachers at Withington Girls' School, in particular Jen Baylis, Sarah Haslam, Diane Whitehead, and Janet Pickering. Laura Firth for all her hard work.

Team Chapman. My parents, to whom I will always be grateful. Rosie, an insightful early reader and great friend. Nick for providing my first rave review ('I wouldn't have read this if my sister hadn't written it.')

My friends. In particular, Kate Yateman-Smith for promising we would run away together. Nemira Gasiunas for softminting and support. Kate Antrobus for endless congratulations cards. Liz Thomas and Ellie Johnston at Wild Lily Empire. Claire Weir for her brilliant photography. Tomek Mossakowski for being my Scandinavian expert.

Ben Mosey, for being himself, and for reminding me that I am not a tap.

picador.com

blog
videos
interviews
extracts